Edward Sylvester Ellis

The River Fugitives

Edward Sylvester Ellis

The River Fugitives

ISBN/EAN: 9783744791298

Printed in Europe, USA, Canada, Australia, Japan

Cover: Foto ©Andreas Hilbeck / pixelio.de

More available books at **www.hansebooks.com**

"A COLONEL SHOULD NEVER ASSUME COMMAND OF ANY BODY WHICH
HE CANNOT CONTROL."—Page 77.

BY

EDWARD S. ELLIS

AUTHOR OF "DEERFOOT" SERIES, "LOG CABIN" SERIES,
"BOY PIONEER" SERIES, ETC.

ILLUSTRATED

PHILADELPHIA

HENRY T. COATES & CO.

CONTENTS.

CHAP.		PAGE.
I—The Wyoming Massacre,		7
II—By the River,		14
III—The Encounter,		21
IV—In the Susquehanna,		28
V—A Dreadful Deed,		38
VI—Gloomy Forebodings,		45
VII—The Forest Rose,		55
VIII—Dangerous Admiration,		62
IX—A Quarrel,		70
X—Rather too Kind,		79
XI—The Plan,		85
XII—A Valuable Ally,		92
XIII—The Flight,		102
XIV—Lena-Wingo Steps to the Front,		109
XV—In the Wilderness,		116
XVI—Queen Esther,		123
XVII—A Struggle for Life,		130
XVIII—A Labyrinth of Peril,		137
XIX—An Enemy and yet a Friend,		144
XX—The Other Duty,		151
XXI—A Strange Escape,		158
XXII—Eight against One,		167
XXIII—An Unexpected Ally,		174
XXIV—Unexpected Peril,		182
XXV—The Spider's Web,		189
XXVI—All Abroad,		196
XXVII—Behind the Trees,		203
XXVIII—The Depth of Sorrow,		210
XXIX—Groping in the Forest,		219
XXX—A Discovery,		226
XXXI—A Test of the Nerves,		234
XXXII—The Occupant of the Canoe,		242
XXXIII—The Consultation,		249

THE RIVER FUGITIVES.

CHAPTER I.

THE WYOMING MASSACRE.

"Look out, Ned, the Indians are as thick and plenty as hornets when you stir up a dozen nests of them; you're running altogether too fast, and you'll be in a trap before you know it."

"What's the use of talking that way, Jo?" demanded his companion, in an impatient voice; "if we hadn't done the hardest kind of running, we would have lost our scalps long ago. I can tell you that I won't feel safe till we've put a good fifty miles behind us, and we see Stroudsburg ahead."

"That's just what we aren't going to see for a good long while. There's many a long mile of woods between Wyoming and Stroudsburg, and the Tories and Indians know that the poor settlers are doing their best to get there and to

Wilkesbarre, and so they'll watch that route more than any other."

At the end of these hurried words, Ned Clinton and Jo Minturn came to a halt, and the former asked, in a frightened and somewhat petulant tone:

"Well, Jo, what do you think is the best thing for us to do?"

"We can't do anything just yet. We are both out of wind, and can't run faster than a man can walk; and so I say we may as well stop and take breath, and look over the ground a little before we try to get out of the neighborhood. Night will soon set in, and, if we are careful, we have a chance of dodging the Tories and Indians."

"A chance of dodging the Tories and Indians?" repeated the other boy. "Why, they are all around, and I don't see much show for us."

These were bitter words, but there was good cause for their utterance. The lad had not exaggerated the terrors of that day, in July, 1778, when it seemed as if a legion of fiends had been loosed, and given full power to work their will all through the lovely valley of Wyoming.

In order to understand the incidents we have taken upon ourselves to relate, we give as briefly as possible the leading facts of one of the most dreadful disasters that marred the struggles of our fathers for independence: In the latter part of the month of June, 1778, Colonel John Butler, of the British army, with about four hundred Provincials, made up of Tories, together with six or seven hundred Indians, entered the head of the Wyoming valley, and took possession of Fort Wintermoot without opposition, they having massacred a number of settlers on the way. Colonel Zebulon Butler, a cousin of the British leader, was on a visit to the valley at the time, and assumed command of all the available forces that could be raised for the defense. His entire force consisted of two hundred and thirty enrolled men, and seventy old people, boys, civil magistrate and others, who, under ordinary circumstances, would be classed as non-combatants. These were all mustered at "Forty Fort"—so called from having been erected by forty Connecticut settlers—where the families on the western side of the river had taken refuge.

"Indian Butler," as he was generally known, summoned the defenders to surrender the fort and the valley. In answer to this peremptory demand, a council of war was held on the third of July, at

which Colonels Butler and Denison and Lieuten-
ant-Colonel Dorrance favored a dallying policy,
in the hope that reinforcements would arrive and
enable them to make the defense successful beyond
a doubt. The larger part of the defenders advo-
cated marching out at once and giving their
enemies battle, confident of their power to rout
them, "horse, foot and dragoons." Butler, a
brave and skillful officer, listened to the clamor
quietly, until he seemed to be impressed with the
belief that this ardor and enthusiasm only needed
directing to carry everything before it.

"The attack shall be made as you wish!" he
exclaimed, as he leaped into the saddle; "and I
shall lead you as far as any dare follow; but
remember you go into great danger, where it is
win all or lose all."

It was near the middle of the afternoon that the
column, numbering about three hundred men, old
men and boys, marched out of the fort, with
drums beating and colors flying. They passed up
the plain, with the Susquehanna on their right
and a marsh on their left, until they reached Fort
Wintermoot, which was in flames. It had been
fired by the enemy in order to give the impression
that they were retiring from the valley. The

ground for the battle was selected by Colonel
Zebulon Butler's aids, and when the position was
taken the right rested on a steep bank, the left
extending across the gravel flat to a morass, thick
with timber and brush, that separated the bottom-
land from the mountain, while yellow and pitch
pine-trees and oak shrubs were scattered all over
the plain.

The battle began at four o'clock in the afternoon. Colonel Butler had impressed his men with
the importance of withstanding the first shock,
and ordered them to fire, and at each discharge to
advance a step. As the fight opened and progressed, the British line gave way, in spite of all
the officers could do to prevent it. The Indians
were engaged from the first, they being on the
British right. They were divided into six bands,
and as they fired, they kept up a series of whoops
and yells of the most frightful character.

It is a sad reflection that a fight which opened so
favorably for the little band of patriots should
soon turn overwhelmingly against them, but such
was the fact. At the end of half an hour the greatly
superior power of the enemy began to develop
itself, the Indians continuing to pour out of the
swamp, in which they had concealed the greater

part of their number, and the left was outflanked
and thrown into confusion. An order to execute
a certain military maneuver was mistaken by
many for a command to fall back, and the con-
flict of movements threw the whole force into
inextricable confusion. Seeing the imminent peril
that threatened, Colonel Butler dashed between
the opposing fires, regardless of his own life, and
shouted to his men that they had only to stand
firm and victory was theirs.

At this critical moment a horde of redskins
swooped down upon the disorganized patriots,
and the stampede was complete. Every captain
that led a company into action was slain. More
than two hundred of the Americans were massacred, the loss of the British and Indians being one-
third as great. Colonels Butler and Denison, being
mounted, succeeded in reaching the fort, conveying
the tidings of what had taken place to the terrified
fugitives huddled together there.

Butler, on account of more than one daring
exploit against the British during the preceding
years of the Revolution, was especially hated by
them, and he knew only too well what his fate
would be if he fell into their hands. Nevertheless,
he remained in the fort until the terms were

arranged that should be offered the enemy on the morrow. He then crossed over to Wilkesbarre, and, throwing a feather-bed on his horse, seated his wife behind, and left the valley the next day. Those who had taken refuge in the Wilkesbarre fort began a precipitate flight the next morning, and as they were unprovided with enough provisions, many women and children perished with fatigue and hunger in a dense pine forest, which is known to this day as "The Shades of Death." The terms proposed to the British Colonel Butler were accepted and signed by him, and the surrender of Forty Fort was made on the fourth of July, 1778. On the succeeding day the Indians began plundering, and when Colonel Denison remonstrated with the British leader, the latter declared that the Indians—many of whom were drunk and committing all sorts of excesses—were beyond his control.

Having thus briefly sketched the leading features of the ever-memorable Wyoming massacre, we take up again the thread of our story.

CHAPTER II.

BY THE RIVER.

AMONG the band of old men and children that issued from "Forty Fort," on the day of the fight at Wyoming were Ned Clinton and Jo Minturn, who were side by side at the opening of the battle, both being in that portion of the command attacked with such fury by the Indians, and that finally became panic-stricken and turned into a complete rout, leading the headlong fight that was the real beginning of the massacre. Young Clinton was about eighteen years of age, and went into the fight, leaving an aged mother at the fort, while his only other relative, an uncle, was shot down and tomahawked before his eyes. Jo Minturn was a year younger than his companion, and alone in the struggle, so far as any of his relatives were concerned; but he left a decrepit father, a mother, and a sister, Rosa, a year younger than himself, so that it will be understood the interests of both were bound up in the little defense itself.

Both the young men, rather curiously, were of

the opinion that all the fugitives in the fort were safe. Perhaps it was not so curious, either, for no one could believe that, in case they were compelled to surrender to Colonel Butler, he would fail to see that they received the fullest and most complete protection. Hence the two friends were engaged in trying to save their own scalps. They had made several essays to reach the fort, but the majority of the fugitives had been massacred, while striving to do the same thing; so they were obliged to turn back again, and were in the woods, near the river, which flowed broad and deep before them.

"It seems to me," said Ned, after they had paused long enough to regain their breath, "that the wisest thing for us to do is to swim across. What do you say?"

"I don't know that it makes much difference whether we do or not, for the redskins are pretty well scattered on both sides by this time, and we're as likely to run against them in one place as another. I've an idea that we could find a good hiding-place on Monacacy island, out there in the river—that is, for a little while."

"But, then, we aren't in want of an extra hiding-place just now; all we have to do is to keep poking and picking our way along till we are so far away from this place that we shall be well clear of the Tories and Indians. I had no idea of staying longer by the way than we have to."

"Nor I, either; the fact is, we can't pick out any spot within a dozen miles of the fort where we aren't liable to run against a lot of enemies. Let's keep on along the river, and if we travel all night we will be so far off by morning that we can feel pretty safe. The folks at the fort will be dreadfully worried over us, won't they?"

"Yes, but we can't help that; they will be sure we are both killed, till they see us with their own eyes."

Having decided what they would do, and having rested themselves so far as to recover their wind, there was no further excuse for their remaining in the neighborhood. The hot summer day had not yet ended, and so they were forced to be extremely careful in moving through the woods, when they were so liable to be seen by some of the black eyes that were peering everywhere in search of victims. Here and there the crack of a rifle was heard, and not a minute passed in which they did not catch the curdling sound of the Indian yell, showing how relentlessly the savages were prose-

cuting their work. The smoke from the ruins of
Fort Wintermoot lay like a great smirch against
the sky, and, here and there, where a glimpse
could be caught of the plain, the massacre was
going on.

The mind can become accustomed almost to anything, and the two young men, who, a few hours
before, were so shocked at seeing an Indian bury
his tomahawk into the brain of a helpless and sup-
plicating old man, had already witnessed so many
equally horrible crimes, that they took them
almost as a matter of course, and busied themselves in doing their utmost to escape. The two
were within a few yards of the river bank, when
Ned Clinton, who was a single step in advance of
his friend, abruptly paused, and raising his hand
in a warning way, uttered the soft exclamation:

"'Sh!"

Jo was on the lookout for something of the
kind, and he checked himself on the instant, the
two standing as motionless as a couple of stone
statues. They scarcely breathed, even, while all
their faculties were centered in the single one of
listening. A minute followed without the silence
in their immediate vicinity being broken, when

2

Jo Minturn ventured to lean a little forward and whisper in the ear of his friend:

"What was it, Ned?"

"Can't say," he answered, in the same cautious voice; "but I am sure I heard something moving through the bushes."

"Likely it is somebody trying to hide, for if it was an Indian, there would be no need of his being so sly about it."

"All right; it was just there in front of where we are standing," added Ned, pointing to a dense mass of undergrowth directly before them. "You turn to the left and I'll go to the right, and we'll move toward each other as soon as we get as near the water as we can. By that means we'll stand a chance of finding out what it is."

The suggestion was acted upon at once. The youths, knowing that a blunder was almost certain to result in their becoming victims to the tomahawk, were as careful and as cautious in their movements as a couple of veteran scouts. Ned Clinton, perhaps by virtue of his prior discovery, seemed to think it was his place to take the lead. As he knew the precise point from which the suspicious sound came, he moved more directly toward it than did his companion.

Enough light still remained for him to see objects a few rods distant with great distinctness. He had not advanced more than five steps when he became convinced that his first supposition was right, for there was certainly some one crouching in the undergrowth immediately in front, and Ned uttered their familiar signal—a soft whistle—as a warning to his friend, a rod or two distant, that he had made an important discovery.

The two had gone into battle with a rifle apiece, and they had brought the weapons away with them; but they had nothing more. All raw troops are apt to use too much powder in battle, and it so happened that the two lads had not a dozen charges left between them, a fact that made them anxious, since they were more cool and collected, to be as economical in the use of their ammunition as possible. It looked to Ned as if he might then find it necessary to spend some powder, and he therefore raised the hammer of his gun, sank down in a crouching posture, and began stealing his way, inch by inch, in the direction of the motionless figure that could be dimly seen through the undergrowth.

"I don't know whether he sees me or not," thought Ned, as he stealthily shoved his rifle

through the grass and bushes in his immediate
front. "But I don't mean that he shall get the
best of me if there is any way to hinder it."

There was a strong suspicion in the mind of Ned
that the figure which he dimly saw hiding was
that of some poor, panic-stricken fugitive, too
much dazed and bewildered by the horrors of the
day to be able to tell a friend from a foe. It was
this suspicion, amounting to almost a belief, that
induced Ned Clinton to forget his motto of Ike
Wells, the old hunter, to the effect that, when on
the scout, every stranger must be set down as an
enemy until he was proved a friend.

"Hello, there?" called out the youth, in a reas-
suring though cautious voice. "We are Americans.
Don't be afraid. Who are you?"

There was some sort of reply made to this which
Ned did not catch, but which threw him completely
off his guard.

"I didn't get what you said," he added, in a still
more incautious voice; "but you can be sure we
are friends, so come out and show yourself."

CHAPTER III.

THE ENCOUNTER.

At this critical juncture Jo Minturn, from his lurking place, only a rod or so away, emitted a low whistle; but the trouble in this case was, that it was a little too cautious. The friend for whom it it was intended heard it not, although his intense curiosity at that particular moment, no doubt, was one reason why he failed to notice that which would have excited his alarm at any other time. It may well be asked how it was that the one who was so much further away should have heard, or, at least, have given, the signal of alarm, when he whose place it was to guard against that very form of danger failed to see it. The answer is, that Jo saw and heard nothing at all; it was merely a suspicion with him, nothing more.

"Are you wounded?" asked Ned, as he neared the crouching form and leaned forward in the hope of identifying him. "If there is anything the matter with you, let me know, and Jo and I will do all we can for you. This is hardly the place—"

To the amazement of the young man, the pros-
trate figure at this instant sprang up with the suddenness of lightning, and gave out that curdling
whoop which he had heard so often while the battle and massacre were going on. The action was
so utterly unexpected that Ned was paralyzed for
the moment, as if he did not comprehend what
had taken place. This was the very artifice that
the Indian had been planning when the youth
detected him moving through the bushes. It succeeded precisely as was intended, the few seconds
of bewilderment and surprise affording the opportunity for the hurling of his tomahawk, as it
seemed that he had expended all his ammunition
before he reached this spot.

In the gathering gloom, Ned saw the swarthy
arm drawn back, and he caught the gleam of the
weapon, as it was raised aloft to strike, or,
rather, to hurl with unerring aim, straight
at his brain. The sweep of the arm and the
glitter of the tomahawk served to arouse Ned
to a sense of his peril, and he made a desperate
attempt to raise his rifle and shoot the savage
before he could drive the deadly missile into his
skull. But he had delayed too long to save himself.

Still, if Ned Clinton had lost his senses, Jo Minturn had not. The latter, from the first, held a suspicion that something was wrong, and so, in a measure had prepared for the very danger that had come upon his friend. At the moment the Indian sprang to his feet Jo read the whole plot, and he cocked his rifle, muffling the sound as much as possible, for he wanted to make the surprise of the miscreant as complete as the latter had made that of the young man, who stood as one dumb before him. But there was no time for delay, for when the Indian got upon his feet and went to work, he was like a panther in his movements.

Jo, therefore, did not tarry. When he saw the muscular arm raised he threw up his rifle, and taking quick aim, fired. The distance was so short that it was hardly possible to miss, and simultaneous with the sharp report of the gun was the wild death-shriek of the savage, who threw his arms in the air and fell forward on his face, with not a spark of life in his body.

"By George, that was well done, Jo!" exclaimed his grateful companion, "and you have saved my life. I stood there transfixed for a moment, just as you were the other day when that rattlesnake got his eyes fixed on you."

"That will do, Ned," replied his friend, in some excitement. "We haven't got time to stop to talk now, but must be moving."

"Why such a desperate hurry, Jo? It is already quite dark, and there are no other Indians in sight."

"They'll be here soon enough, you may depend on that."

"And how do you make that out?" asked his companion, as he followed him down closer to the river.

"Didn't you hear that yell he let out just as he rose, and drew back to let you have his toma-hawk? Well, you can make up your mind that half a dozen or more heard that, too, and they'll flock to this spot like so many wolves when one of their number signals to the others that he has found a choice bit of prey."

"You're right, Jo. And we must get out of this place—"

"'Sh! not so loud," whispered his companion; "they're coming now."

The speaker was right. Both heard, at the instant, a soft, low sound, like the chirp of a bird, and which they knew was a call, intended to be answered by the Indian that had just fallen by the rifle of Jo Minturn. For obvious reasons, the proper response could not be made to this, and the only wise thing for the young men to do was to vacate the position with as little delay as possible.

There was not much to be feared from the report of the avenging rifle, as reports were sounding at intervals from all parts of the bloody plain. But, as Jo had declared, it was the result of that yell which they must guard against. Beyond all question, one or more redskins were stealing upon them, and Ned and Jo, as they reached the edge of the Susquehanna, knelt down and stepped into the water.

"Shall we swim across?" asked the latter, in a whisper.

"We'll have to go out into the river, anyway, for if we move up or down, we are sure to be headed off, but it is best to halt on the island. I don't believe there are many there, and there are plenty of places where we can hide till it becomes darker, and then we'll pull out and strike for the shore again."

"All right; here we go."

They were not a moment too soon, for as they waded out a little farther in the stream, they heard the same signal that had attracted their suspicion at first. But this time it sounded directly behind them, from the very spot that they had occupied but a short time before. The Indians were there, and it seemed almost impossible that the two fugitives should escape observation.

It occurred to both that there was less danger of being seen if they separated, and, without a word, they sank down until only enough of their heads remained above to permit them to breathe. Then they began moving noiselessly through the water in the direction of Monacacy island, the outlines of which were barely visible. Their rifles very nearly caused their betrayal, as it was necessary that they should be shifted over their shoulders, so as to allow them the unrestricted use of their arms.

Ordinarily, this was a very slight piece of work, executed in a minute or so, but the labor was immeasurably increased when they were in the water, where they were not only anxious to do it in a guarded manner, but at the same time to keep the stocks above their heads, so that the weapons would be ready for use when they should leave the river again. Both succeeded better than they had reason to expect, and diverging, they swam toward the island which had become, for the time being, a land of refuge to them. Their paths were so far apart that they almost immediately lost sight of each other, and each went on his own hook.

Ned Clinton had no more than gotten fairly under way, after adjusting his gun, when he heard the Indian signal repeated for the third time, and, with a shiver of dismay, he caught a sound that he was sure was made by some one entering the water.

"As sure as I live they have started after us," he muttered, as he increased his speed, not forgetting to work his way with the stealth that he had used at the beginning.

At the same moment he glanced over his shoulder, toward the place he had just left. It may have been fancy, and it may have been fact, but he was quite sure that he saw several dark forms in the act of entering the water, and, of course, for no other purpose than to pursue him and his friend.

CHAPTER IV.

IN THE SUSQUEHANNA.

WHETHER Ned really saw the Indians or not, as they entered the river behind him, is a small matter. Within the succeeding three minutes he became certain that he was pursued by the very beings from whom he and his friend had been fleeing for the last hour or more. The Indians had found the dead body of their former comrade, and understood what it meant. Some of the whites had managed to escape, in spite of the persistency with which the invaders had kept up the massacre, and they were now inspired by the feeling of revenge, added to their own natural cruelty of heart.

Ned would have felt little fear of a single Indian, had he been permitted to meet him under anything like equal conditions; but he was confident that several were after him. Even if there was only one, it would have been a piece of folly for him to engage in a personal encounter, so long as there was a possibility of avoiding it. Ned naturally concluded that the redskins would think that he

28

was making for the island, where so many had already taken refuge, and in the hope of misleading them, he turned and struck out for a point below the land itself.

Having progressed a few rods in this manner, he held up, for the purpose of learning what his enemies were doing. The young man was a splendid swimmer, and he had no fear that, if it were necessary, he could keep himself afloat an hour or more. It was quite dark by this time, for which he was thankful; for had the Indians been able to see them from the shore, they would have ended the tragedy, so far as the two friends were concerned, by sending a bullet through the head of each.

Supporting himself with only his nose and eyes in the air, Ned looked anxiously back toward the shore he had left but a few minutes before. For a brief space he saw nothing; but, as all swimmers know, sound is carried with greater distinctness under than above the water, and he heard the soft rustling noise which is an invariable accompaniment of the most skillful swimmer's efforts when making his way ever so cautiously through the current.

"They are coming, that's certain," muttered Ned, still holding himself motionless, and using his sight and hearing as best he could. "They will pass me very near, but they can't hear me, I am sure, and I hope they won't see me, either."

The thought had scarcely taken shape in the mind of the fugitive, when he caught sight of what looked like a cocoanut moving over the surface of the water, and which he was certain was the "cocoanut" of one of his pursuers. That was more than enough, and he quietly dropped out of sight altogether, and swam several yards beneath before coming to the surface.

When the distended blood-vessels could bear no more, he pushed his nose upward, took in a draught of the life-sustaining air, and looked about him. The first glance disclosed the head about as near as before, and he was wondering how that could be, when he reflected that it was not the one from which he fled, but a second Indian, following a little to the right of the former.

"So there are two of you," he said to himself, edging away, without going under a second time. "Yes, and there comes a third, and there is no telling how many more."

Poising himself like an eagle over the mountain crag, he waited and watched, ready at any moment to drop under again, the instant it should appear necessary. His purpose was to find out the precise number of their pursuers, and he ran a great risk in order to do so; but after waiting several minutes without detecting any more, he made up his mind that he had seen the last.

"Just three," he muttered, as he cautiously resumed his swimming in the same course followed by them. "That wouldn't make a very uneven sort of a fight, if we could meet them on a fair field; but the first thing they would do when they caught sight of us would be to let out a yell that would bring half a hundred down on us; so I guess we'll give them the go-by, if they will let us."

He paused, for at that moment his trained ear caught a repetition of the sound that had alarmed him, and told him that some one was in the water near him. Ned accepted this as a warning that he was treading too close, so to speak, on the heels of his red enemies, and he slackened his efforts, which were so slight in the first place. Still the rustling continued, and he looked anxiously ahead in the gloom, and was unable to distinguish anything of the swimmer who, as was very evident, must be the cause of this same slight noise.

"That's queer," he thought. "According to that sound, he is pretty close by, and yet I'll be shot if I can see anything of his head on the water."

Long and bitter experience teaches the brave man to become the skillful, patient and successful scout, and Clinton was in the act of receiving a lesson that would never be forgotten. Strange, that in peering round in the gloom for the author of the slight but excessively annoying sound, proving beyond all doubt that one of his dreaded enemies was somewhere close at hand, it did not occur to him that it might proceed from the most dangerous point of all—behind him. Yet such was the fact. Ned's faculties were strung to that pitch that he noticed the peculiar increase in the rustling that showed that it was approaching.

"I wonder whether he is swimming *under* the water?" he asked himself with a shudder, as the redskin still failed to show up. "If he comes at me that way, it will be hard work."

With the suddenness of the lightning's flash the whole truth burst upon. The Indian was approaching from *behind*. Turning his head, Ned saw him so near that he was in the very act of raising his hand to bury his bloody knife into his shoulder. The white youth was without any knife, and his gun was of no use to him. That which the endangered fugitive did was the result of instinct more than reason.

He sank beneath the surface, doing it so quickly and cleverly that the blow of the Indian was frustrated, and the savage knew not where to feel for him. Under such circumstances, he did what was the most natural. He waited for him to rise, holding the weapon aloft, ready to complete his work at the very moment the head came within reach. The savage must have felt sure of his victim, for he did not utter that yell which comes so natural to all of his kind when they catch sight of a foe, and think it possible they may need a little assistance in disposing of him.

But when Ned Clinton went beneath the surface of the stream he felt that his life depended upon his doing something more than merely diving. The redskin was seeking his death, and the time had come for him to prove what he was made of. Which is precisely what he did do; for, without a moment's hesitation, he struck out the instant he was under, not away from but toward his foe.

The two were so close that only a stroke or two was required to bring them in collision. The Delaware was looking keenly around in the gloom for his victim, when his legs were suddenly seized near the knees, and he was jerked under. Being an Indian he was a good swimmer; but the most skillful of Paul Boytons may be taken off his guard. The redskin, as he dipped below, gave a gasping inspiration that was the worst thing he could do, for it caused him to "ship" a large amount of water, and, scarcely knowing what it meant for the first second, he made such a frantic clawing of the arms that the knife dropped therefrom. He was placed on the same footing as his assailant so far as weapons were concerned, while he was temporarily at a disadvantage, owing to the flurry in which he was thrown by the strange manner in which he had been assailed.

Fortunately, Ned Clinton comprehended his vantage-ground in this respect, and he possessed the sense to use it, without an instant's delay, which, probably, would have wrested it from his grasp. He aimed to keep the Indian under until he should drown, as there was every reason to believe he could do. The preliminary strangling that the Delaware had undergone contributed

materially to this end. When Ned felt the vigorous savage growing weaker in his grasp, he was
strengthened by the fact, and, almost strangling
to death himself, he still kept the hot poisoned
air in his throbbing lungs, until he shoved the
brawny wretch still lower, and succeeded in raising himself upon his shoulders into the life restor-
ing air above.

With the inhalation came renewed strength and
confidence, and he forced the Indian still lower,
holding him there with the strength of a giant.
In a few seconds all was still; but Ned did not let
th· redskin up, fearing that he was counterfeiting
death, so as to throw him off his guard. But in
a few more moments the Delaware became quiet,
as if made of lead. Then he dropped still lower,
and was seen no more.

"I got along a good deal easier with him than
I expected," murmured Ned, as he resumed his
careful and deliberate swim in the direction of the
island.

The purpose of the fugitive was now to join Jo
Minturn, who had preceded him to Monacacy,
and for whose safety he was greatly concerned, on
account of the trio of Indians whom he had seen
following after him. Common prudence would

have dictated another course. Knowing that the
island was swarming with Indians and Tories,
all engaged in searching it from one end to the
other for victims, there surely was little to com-
mend in the way of a refuge. But the fact that
Jo Minturn was there was enough to lead Ned in
the same direction; for the two had been bosom
friends from their earliest boyhood, and, when
they marched out of Forty Fort that hot summer afternoon, it was the determination of both
to stand by each other to the death. Leaving
this profound friendship out of view, there was
another powerful reason that would have led Ned
Clinton in the same course, and that was the fact
that Jo was the brother of Rosa Minturn,—but
of that hereafter. The young man was quite confident that he had command of his own actions,
and although the other redskins might miss the
warrior, it was not likely that they would attrib-
ute his disappearance to the right cause and
seek to avenge it.

"Jo will be looking out for me and I for him,
and both of us for the redskins, so we ought to
be able to take care of ourselves—hello!"

At this moment, when the swimmer was beginning to felicitate himself on the shape matters

were taking, he was alarmed by seeing the heads of three Indians who had passed by him when he halted and waited for the fourth warrior. It was plain from this that they were expecting the one who was never to come; and the instant Ned caught sight of them, they also detected him, for one of them uttered an exclamation that was intended as a sort of summons.

Ned did not lose his self-possession under these trying circumstances, but as he was barely visible, with his identity as yet unsuspected, he once more sank out of sight, and by a few vigorous movements, placed himself so far beyond the point where he went down that he was beyond the range of their vision when he came up again. This fortunate advantage he increased with as much celerity as was compatible with his own safety.

CHAPTER V.

A DREADFUL DEED.

For awhile, matters went a great deal more smoothly with Jo Minturn than they did with his old friend, who had fallen behind in the swim for Monacacy island. As they had set out to reach this island it seemed to Jo that the sooner they did so the better it would be for them. Accordingly, after he struck out and was fairly under way, he kept straight ahead, even though it was apparent that several Indians were only a short distance in the rear, in hot pursuit. Jo was quite sure that he could make his way through the water as rapidly as any of his pursuers, and for this reason he kept it up, although his friend Ned was beyond his sight.

The result looked as if Jo had taken the wiser course after all; for the actions of Ned kept the little company of Delaware Indians longer in the water than would have been the case had they sped straight onward in pursuit. And so it came about that, when Jo touched bottom and was ready to begin wading, he paused and looked searchingly around, and saw nothing at all of his enemies.

"Beat them swimming after all," with a little natural pride over his imagined exploit. "It's a pity Ned didn't do the same, instead of waiting, in the belief that he can outwit them. I am satisfied that we must have a little more experience before it will be safe for us to try to beat the savages and Tories at that game."

The young man was in doubt for a moment or two as to whether he should stay where he was and wait for his companion, or withdraw a little from the shore. But it occurred to him that the pursuing Delawares were likely to leave the water at that same point—in which event his situation would prove anything but a safe one. He therefore moved back a step or two, where in case it became necessary, he could avail himself of the shelter of the undergrowth.

He was not a moment too soon in doing so. He had just reached the spot when the figure of a man rose from the water less than a rod distant and hurried into the bushes a few yards from the shore, where he sank down like one who was hiding from pursuers. The precise point at which he emerged was a dozen feet below where Jo was standing, and the first emotion of the young scout on seeing him was that of surprise that he had failed to observe him when he was in the river itself.

The incident taught him the wisdom of his action in withdrawing from his exposed position. Jo was convinced that the man was one of the fugitives trying to escape from the Tories and Indians, but where the situation was so critical, he hesitated to approach or hail him, and it was well he did so refrain. For the individual, whose manner showed that he was wearied and exhausted, had scarcely dropped into his hiding-place, when his pursuer, also unseen by the young scout, stepped from the river and proceeded in a direct line toward him. This man was also white, and the inference was fair that he was a Tory—one of those renegades as cruel and merciless as their copper-colored allies —without the same palliation for their diabolical enmity of the settlers of Wyoming valley.

"If that's your game," muttered Jo, "I'll take a hand in the business myself, for I can stand seeing a white man killed by an Indian better than looking at a white man slaying one of his own race."

Jo unslung his rifle from his back, and brought it round to the front, so that it would be ready for instant use, and he followed the wretch with the stealthy tread of an Indian. Enough light remained for him to distinguish the Tory searching the bushes and undergrowth for the fugitive, who must have watched his approach with the most poignant feelings of terror. Guided by a cruel fate, the Tory gradually neared the hiding-place of the fugitive, who, seeing that discovery was inevitable, came forth and threw himself on his knees before his enemy.

"Spare me, Brother John!" pleaded the terrified fugitive, for it was his own brother to whom he was kneeling—"spare me, and I will be your servant as long as I live!"

"That is all very well," was the inhuman reply, "but what business have you to be a rebel?"

"I was only fighting for my family and my home, and we have been defeated and enough of our people killed."

"Not while one of the rebels still lives; there has not half of them been killed yet."

"You surely wouldn't kill your own brother, John! Let me live, and I will do anything in the world for—"

Further words were cut short forever by the explosion of the rifle almost against the head of the poor wretch, who fell backward, killed by the bullet of his own brother. And just here—lest our readers may think we are indulging in unwarrantable exaggeration—we may state that the incident just given is a fact as clearly established as the massacre of Wyoming itself. The name of the fratricide was John Pencil, and of his brother, Henry. It is said that the Indians themselves were shocked at the unnatural crime, as they well might be. There is something instructive in the subsequent fate of the fratricide, which is also strictly authentic.

The crime was so atrocious that it became known to all the survivors of the fight, and John Pencil never dared to return to Wyoming valley; but, after the Revolution, went to Canada, where he settled in the wilderness with a number of other refugees. While living here, he was twice chased by wolves, and on each occasion was saved by the Indians. The superstitious redskins at last came to believe that a retributive fatality was following him, and they refused to go to his assistance when he was beset a third time by the ravenous beasts of the forest, and a short while after he was set upon again, and literally torn to pieces and devoured by the howling wolves—fit end for such a miscreant.

And what was Jo Minturn doing while this frightful crime was being perpetrated? When he comprehended that the two men were really brothers, he could not believe the fugitive was in danger; but as the few words that passed between them foreshadowed the atrocious crime, he raised his own gun with the resolve to shoot the Tory before he could fire. The aim was taken and the trigger drawn, but the dull click that followed proved that his ammunition had become so wet during his swim in the Susquehanna that it was useless. But, impelled by his burning horror, he raised the hammer and aimed, and pulled the trigger again, only to be chagrined beyond measure by a second failure. Ere he could repair the error the fatal shot was fired, and the deed done before his eyes.

Determined that the monster should not escape the death that he had earned, Jo clubbed his gun with the purpose of braining him where he stood; but at this critical moment the young patriot dis-

covered that he had been seen by several Indians,
who were so close upon him that his danger was
greater than at any time during the terrible fight
and massacre.   Nothing but instant flight could
save him.

CHAPTER VI.

GLOOMY FOREBODINGS.

SUCH being the case, Jo made a desperate attempt to elude his sleepless enemies by a tremendous leap to one side, and a furious run for the river, which was but a short distance away. Like most of the young men of his day and neighborhood, he was very active upon his feet, as one needed to be who ran a race with a party of Delawares or Mohawks. The fugitive was only a short distance from the water, but he took a diagonal course, so as to keep in the shelter of the undergrowth as long as possible, his belief being that by this means he could secure a chance to double, and perhaps to leave the redskins behind.

The young scout was seen at the instant he started, as he was apprised by a series of shouts and yells, telling that the pursuers were close at his heels. Jo, however, was well acquainted with the length and breadth of Monacacy island, and thus at the beginning he possessed a slight advantage over his pursuers. That availed him scarcely anything, unfortunately, as they kept so close to his heels that it seemed impossible for him to dodge out of sight even for an instant. But, for all that, Jo Minturn escaped his pursuers by a means that was as singular as it was rare.

He was running with might and main, when it struck him that his only chance would be by making a running leap into the Susquehanna. With this purpose in view he made a sudden and sharp turn toward the river, but had taken scarcely a step when he caught his foot in some sort of a vine, and he fell violently to the ground. Almost on the very spot where he fell was another fugitive in hiding. This poor fellow supposed that his enemies had detected him, and, with a cry of terror, he sprang to his feet, and dashed off for dear life, the redskins keeping on directly after him, without any suspicion of the manner in which the identity of the two had been changed.

The only thing that prevented their discovery of the curious fact was the partial stunning that Jo received. It caused him to lie motionless long enough for the Indians to pass by him in their pursuit of the man who ought to have lain still where he was resting when he was broken in upon so unexpectedly. With quick returning consciousness came to Jo the perception of what had taken place, and he was grateful indeed; resolved, too, that the advantage thus gained should not be thrown away by any subsequent indiscretion of his.

Cautiously rising to his feet, he looked around and listened. Gazing across to the shore, and up and down the valley, he still saw the glare of burning buildings, and heard the crack of the death-dealing rifles. Ever and anon he caught the savage yell of some of the Indians who were sweeping up and down the valley in search of more victims, their inhuman thirst nourished by what it fed upon. Looking in whatever direction he chose, there was little to attract in the way of a refuge from danger.

The whites were fleeing for life on both sides the river, and there were many in hiding on Monacacy island where he was resting himself for a few minutes. The only course that promised anything at all like safety was in long and continued flight—that is, until they should pass beyond the neighborhood altogether. That he would not hesitate a moment to do, if he could only secure the company of his friend, Ned Clinton, from whom he had parted in the Susquehanna. How to rejoin him was the question he was revolving in his own mind. Troublesome thoughts were beginning to disturb the young fugitive—fears which, until then had had no opportunity to make their existence known.

"What more probable than that Ned has fallen by the hands of some of the Tories and Indians! Our poor folks are lying dead everywhere in the bushes, on both shores of this island, and their bodies are floating down the river for miles. The ground must be covered all the way between here and Forty Fort, and I wonder how things are looking there."

In the last sentence he gave utterance to a dread that had been creeping into his heart for the last half hour, seeming to be stronger as it reappeared after some of the frightful perils through which he was compelled to fight his way.

"I remember that the fate of the fort depends on us; and as we have been utterly routed, of course the fort must go to-morrow. That will place everything in the hands of Colonel John Butler, and I *hope* the folks will be safe, but I can't feel sure of it."

This was the terror that had been gradually growing ever since the defeat of the patriot troops in the valley, and which was such a torment to the young man. Very naturally he tried to argue himself into the belief that his fears were unfounded.

"I suppose that maybe he couldn't keep these Indians and Tories back, after the flight of our men," continued Jo, without succeeding in convincing himself that such was the case; "but when the fort surrenders, it will be to him and his white soldiers. The colonel will then be in a position to make his wishes respected, and he will see to it that no excesses are allowed. There are old men, women and children, and such of the fugitives as have managed to dodge the Indians and Tories so there will be nothing done but the surrender because there is nothing else to do. But *after* the surrender—what then?"

This was the question that constantly presented itself, and which he could not answer in any way that tended to quiet his anxiety. Jo knew, as well as did everybody else, that his sister Rosa, who was at the fort with her mother and decrepit father, was of such beauty of form and feature that she would attract attention anywhere, and much more among a band of Tories and renegades, commanded by such a man as Colonel

John Butler. Jo had more than suspected for
some time past that Ned Clinton looked with
affectionate reverence upon his beautiful sister,
and there was none to whom he would have seen
her betrothed with more genuine pleasure than to
him. He was a soldier in the Continental army,
or, rather, was about to be; for, a native of
Wyoming, and attached to one of the most
widely respected patriot families of the place,
he was on the point of starting out to join the
army under Washington, when he was induced to
wait awhile by the danger that impended over
the valley.

If Ned held Rosa Minturn in such exalted
esteem, he had not revealed it to any one, not
even to her; but Jo, who was his constant companion, had such good opportunity to discover
the truth that he would have been blind had he
failed to do so. But he, too, kept it to himself,
only helping matters along in a sly way by some
insinuating remark in the presence of his sister
relating to the bravery and nobility of character of Ned. Jo was considerably smaller in size
than Ned, and it was arranged that he should
enter the military service of his country in a
year. In the present emergency he was only too

eager to do his utmost for the defense of his own loved ones. But Ned was also young, and he could afford to wait awhile before making his love known to her whom he regarded as above any of her kind upon the broad earth. It was time for war, and he would spend the interval until peace should come again in proving himself worthy of her love.

"Colonel Butler," continued the youth, referring to the British commander, "is a regular officer, and will act as such, for he has a reputation behind him, and is responsible to higher authorities."

He recalled that the leader of the British forces a year or two previous, when the Revolution broke out, was a government functionary under Sir William Johnson. When he fled to Canada, his family fell into the hands of the patriots, and were exchanged for the wife and children of Colonel Campbell, of Cherry valley. He was exceedingly active in the wars on the border, and commanded a regiment of rangers in conjunction with Brandt and his Mohawks, and he was a dreadful scourge to the patriots of Tryon county. It would seem, therefore, in spite of the savage nature of the British leader, that the women and refugees in Forty Fort were in no personal danger; but, to bring the matter down to a fine point, Jo dreaded the effect of the beauty of Rosa upon Butler and his associates.

War is barbarous, as the patriots had already learned, and what was to hinder Colonel Butler, if he took a fancy to the forest beauty, from claiming her as his share of the spoils of the victory? The question was a dreadful one, in all its suggestiveness, but at the same time it was one that Jo felt must be met, and, if possible, answered promptly.

"It will be just like those redcoats to pick up Rosa and run off with her, for there is nothing to hinder them, if they want to do so, and there can't be any doubt that lots of them will be smitten with her the minute she shows herself. Ah! if only the old scout Ike Wells was here, or I don't know but I would just as lief have 'Red Jack the Mohawk;' for he is a good friend of ours, and knows how to circumvent the redskins better than any white man can. But what's the use of wishing?" added the young scout, rousing at the perils that must be met promptly, if at all. "I might stand here all night or for a week and do nothing but wish, and that is all the good it would do me.

I think I'll try to reach the fort, and see what can
be done. Wells is off somewhere with Washington, I suppose, in New Jersey, so it's no use of
looking for him here, and Red Jack is on duty up
in New York state, I believe; so we must depend
on Heaven and ourselves."

He walked cautiously a few steps in the direction of the river, and then paused and listened.
The same sounds were in the air, but he had
become accustomed to them, and was listening for
evidences of danger closer at hand. Everything
in his immediate vicinity was still; and, though
there might be a skulking Delaware or Mohawk
within arm's length, he made up his mind to shift
his quarters without any more delay.

His anxiety was to find his friend, Ned Clinton,
and, with that object in view, he picked his way
with great care to the side of the island com-
manding a partial view of the river which he
had left but a short time before, and where he
hoped still to see his comrade swimming cautiously
toward him. Looking out on the dark surface of
the mildly flowing stream, he stood for several
minutes as motionless as the broad stone upon
which one of his feet was resting. If anyone were
within a rod or so he was quite sure of detecting

him; but the most searching scrutiny failed to
show anything upon which he could build any
hope.

"Ned must know that I did all I could to reach
the island, and that if I am anywhere above
ground I must be here. I hope that nothing has
happened to him."

Any one would suppose that Jo would have felt
greatly concerned for the safety of his comrade,
and it cannot be denied that he was anxious; but
at the same time he had an abiding faith in the
skill as well as the bravery of the daring young
scout, who had shown what he could do over and
over again, when encompassed by peril on every
hand.

"Hello, Ned, is that you?" suddenly asked the
watcher in a guarded undertone, as a figure
appeared at his side from the water."

"I believe so," was the reply, as his friend joined
him. "I propose that we now try to reach the
fort to see how the folks are."

"I am with you," was the glad response.

CHAPTER VII.

THE FOREST ROSE.

THE morning succeeding the massacre of Wyoming rose bright and beautiful over the lovely valley, which looked all the more frightful from the appalling scenes it had witnessed but a few hours before. Within Forty Fort were consternation and distress; for of all the representatives of the numerous settlers there was scarcely one who had not to mourn the loss of some father, brother or son, who had marched out the day before, to the music of drum and fife, with heart beating high with patriotic resolve, and bounding with the belief that the horde of redskins and Tories were to be routed and scattered like chaff by the whirl-wind. And those who remained behind, to watch and pray for the success of the brave defenders, could not but share in a large degree this confidence.

How woeful beyond description, then, was the disappointment that was borne to them, when a few terrified and bleeding fugitives came rushing

back with word that the patriots were routed,
and the invaders were ravaging the valley and
massacring all upon whom they could lay hands!
We pass over the horrors of that ghastly night,
when the weeping and helpless ones watched all
through the long dark hours for the coming of
those who were never to come again; but who,
even while their loved and sorrowing ones were
looking and hoping against hope, were either
struggling vainly against the foe or more merci-
fully, perhaps, were already beyond the power of
torture and pain.

As has been stated, Colonel Denison proffered
to the Tory Butler the terms of surrender, that
Colonel Zebulon Butler had drawn up the night
before, previous to his flight to Wilkesbarre. We
have a copy of these articles of capitulation
before us as we write. The articles are seven in
number, and substantially agree that the settlers,
upon condition of surrendering to the chivalrous
representative of his majesty, King George III.,
shall be allowed to occupy their farms peaceably,
and the lives "of the inhabitants shall be preserved
entire and unhurt." To these articles of capitulation the name of John Butler, the British colonel,

and Nathan Denison, the patriot commander, are attached.

In accordance with this agreement, the gates of the fort were thrown open, and Butler, at the head of the Rangers, and a Seneca chief at the head of the Indians, marched in. The arms of the men were stacked, and given by Butler as a present to the Indians with the remark, "See what a present the Yankees have made you."

Among the patriots in the fort at this time were Lorimer Minturn, a gentleman of means, but so old and decrepit that he was physically unable to march out with the force that went forth to battle. He had insisted upon bearing a gun, and taking part in the fight, but, when Colonel Butler saw his helplessness, he refused to allow him to go with them, and so, much against his will, he was compelled to remain behind. With him were his wife, Susan, and his daughter, Rosa. By a curious combination of circumstances, all the relatives of Ned Clinton were fortunately absent at this critical period, on a visit to some of their connections in Wilkesbarre.

A hundred years ago the Wyoming valley contained, as it does now, some of the sweetest and fairest daughters the sun ever shone upon, and there was no one who was sweeter and fairer than the young and beautiful Rosa Minturn.

She was the twin of her brother and therefore about seventeen; but in mind, in amiability, in grace of movement, and, indeed, in all the charms that make womanhood so winning and attractive, she was all that is seen in those whose years outnumber hers. The lustrous blue eyes; the wealth of waving hair, as black and glossy as the raven's wing; the pearly teeth; the tint of the rounded cheeks; the willowy frame; the musical voice and laugh,—these, added to a simplicity of character and an indescribable charm of manner, made Rosa Minturn a girl who could not fail to attract attention, and win admiration, no matter where, or under what circumstances, she might be seen.

There was only one person in the Wyoming valley who was insensible of the beauty of Rosa, and that was herself—certainly the most appropriate one that could have been named. True, some ardent admirer now and then gave expression to the wonder excited by her remarkable attractiveness; but the forest beauty accepted the florid compliments more in the light of a general acknowledgment to her sex than as a personal tribute to herself.

On the day of the surrender Rosa was busy passing to and fro with her parents, and striving to wean her mind from the contemplation of the horrors of the past and present by interesting herself in the details of the yielding up of the fort.

In one respect she and her folks had been favored above most of those who were in the refuge with them. They had received intelligence from one of the settlers, in whom they placed implicit trust, that the son and brother Jo, in company with Ned Clinton, had succeeded in making off when it became apparent that the fortunes of the day were turned irretrievably against them and they could accomplish no good by staying and fighting longer. Confirmed in so much good tidings, the parents and friends found it very easy to believe that the young scouts were able to take care of themselves, and they were confident that the two had reached some place of safety long before.

All the hum and buzz of the surrender were under way, and Rosa was standing a little apart, gazing upon the scene and occasionally exchanging a word with her mother, seated near, as to their own arrangements for taking up their quarters again in their own home. It was natural that she should feel some interest in the British Colonel Butler, and when he was pointed out to her, she scrutinized him more closely than any one else, with the exception of the Seneca chief that led the Indians into the fort.

If there were better-looking men than Colonel Butler, there were also worse-appearing, from which it will be inferred that he was a person without any very striking characteristics of appearance, which was the fact. He showed a slight inclination to corpulency, though not enough to disfigure him, as his military training had imparted a quickness of movement not usually seen in one who had reached middle life; but no one could look upon the face of the Briton by adoption, without being unfavorably impressed, for there were signs not of coarseness alone, but of positive cruelty of disposition. More than one settler, when he met for the first time the cousin of the leader of the patriots, wondered how it was that he agreed to receive the surrender of the fort at all, for he seemed to be one who would enjoy the braining of the helpless women and children as much as Thayen-danaga, the Indian chief, himself.

Colonel Butler, the Tory, wore no beard, except-ing that which had grown within two or three days; his nose was large and unshapely; his under jaw heavy and suggestive of his combative, bulldog disposition; his face broad, especially between the eyes, so that in this respect he bore considerable resemblance to a common type of the cruel Indian. Add to the "points" already mentioned the coarseness of the skin, which, to one standing near, suggested the ravages of small-pox, the cold, piggish appearance of the eyes, and a set of shaggy, broken teeth, and our readers have all that is necessary to say of his personal appearance.

CHAPTER VIII.

DANGEROUS ADMIRATION.

Rosa Minturn, as we have already said, was standing somewhat apart in the fort, watching the details of the surrender, as they passed under her own eyes, the time not having come as yet in which her own folks should make their preparations to return to their home. It seemed to her, since the terms of the capitulation had been agreed to, that there was no need of further delay; but her father simply replied that they would wait until matters settled down a little, and most of the Indians should depart.

And just there the old gentleman was wise, for his experience in the French and Indian war had given him a knowledge of the character of the Indian, which he could not forget at a critical time. He doubted very much whether his family and those around him were safe anywhere just then, but he was quite confident that the fort came nearer supplying that protection than any other place they could select, which was the reason for his staying there.

At the moment when the eye of Rosa was first arrested by the figure of Colonel Butler, the latter was standing just outside the fort, with his arms folded, in conversation with Colonel Denison, from whom he had received the surrender of the post. The Tory was somewhat the taller, and seemed to look down and listen to the words of the patriot, who was talking quite vigorously. The latter gesticulated very freely, swinging his arms almost in the face of his listener, while his eyes snapped with anger.

Colonel Denison was protesting against the outrages committed by the Tories and Indians with all the dignity of outraged manhood. The face of Colonel Butler was marked by a cynical smile, that had been there for several minutes, so that it resembled that which is seen upon the face of a man suffering from a cramp, the main difference in this case being that there was a grim, sardonic expression, as if the conqueror was rather pleased than otherwise at the accounts of the numerous atrocities that were being poured into his ears. Finally, he yawned, as if growing tired.

"Well, well, colonel," he said, with the grin still there, and displaying his tobacco-stained teeth, "these things must happen, you know, and why make such a rumpus about them?"

"I don't see why they need take place at all," was the instant response of the patriot. "If civilized nations must go to war, there is no reason why they should transform themselves into barbarians!"

"Well, no, you would think not, but the thing can't always be helped, you know. It is you who have committed the greatest blunder."

"How is that?"

"By rising in rebellion against King George, one of the most humane and Christian monarchs the sun ever shone upon."

The countenance of Denison flamed up, for he could not but regard these words in the light of an insult, when the respective situations of these participants were borne in mind. Military officers, as a rule, are not noted for the sweetness of their dispositions, and hot words came to the lips of the patriot. But he suppressed them, under the reflection that the safety of the women, men, and children might be very easily involved in the indiscretion of their commander.

"It will be easier to decide as to who has made the mistake when a few more years shall have passed."

"No one but a fool can doubt the complete extinguishment of this rebellion within a year or so from now."

"It happens, then, that the country abounds with fools, and the number seems likely to increase."

"It has always been the case. I have no doubt that if the people were left free to say what they wished, they would declare the rebels should lay down their arms, and that ragamuffin of yours, Washington, ought to be hanged so high that all the world might see him, and remember the lesson. He will soon be caught, and made to dangle between heaven and earth."

It would require a man of a very sluggish nature, or one whose patriotism was dead, to listen to such a slur upon one of the greatest and best men the world ever knew—he who was "first in war, first in peace, and first in the hearts of his countrymen." Had the two officers been alone, or had the fate of no one beside himself depended on the result of Colonel Denison's words and actions, he would

5

have checked the slur, ere it was finished, with a blow.

"It is idle for you and me to discuss this question," replied Denison, holding his anger down as best he could. "I concede to you the right to do your own thinking, and claim the same prerogative for myself. We are banded together in a solemn compact to fight to the end for our liberties, and we do not believe merely, but we *know*, that we are performing a high duty before heaven. If it is possible for you to think you do right to enslave us, why, I will do my best to fancy that you are not particularly to blame for your clouded understanding. As to Washington, I cannot listen to any reflection upon him from *anyone*."

It would be impossible to describe or picture the intense passion with which this patriotic but daring declaration was made. Denison spoke in a low voice, rather lower, in fact, than usual, only varying the ominous undertone by a slight emphasis; but, as he uttered his reply, he looked straight into the eye of the Tory, and there was a lurking, quivering fire in his own eye, such as is seen in the orb of the jungle tiger when he crouches for his fatal spring. Colonel Butler gazed into the countenance of the officer with an expression of disgust, but there was something that so "backed up" the daring words, that he held down the exasperating expression that was on the end of his tongue. Instead, thereof, he laughed.

"See here, my fiery rebel, what's the use of you and me talking over a matter that we can never agree upon if we keep it up to the crack of doom? I have a question that I want to ask you."

"I am ready to hear it," responded Denison, appreciating the wisdom of the Tory in steering clear of the collision that was so imminent.

"For the last ten minutes or so, I have noticed a young lady standing off yonder who has kept her eye upon me pretty steadily. In short, she shows very plainly that there is something about me which has caught her notice. Don't look too suddenly, for I don't want to stop her pleasant occupation. Who is she?"

The cooling indignation of Colonel Denison was instantly turned to disgust at hearing a married man speak in the style of one who was not too old to be his own daughter. Nevertheless, he chose to give the insolent information asked for.

"That young lady is Miss Rosa Minturn, the

daughter of one of the most prominent citizens of Wyoming."

At the moment of making this reply, the speaker purposely fixed his eyes upon the fair object, in such a pointed way that she could not fail to understand that she was the one who was referred to.

"You ought to have been more careful, colonel," said Butler, in an impatient tone. "She has taken the alarm, and is walking away."

"Like all pure-minded young ladies, she is embarrassed to find herself the object of admiration."

"She is certainly a remarkable beauty."

"And as good as she is handsome," added Denison, who would not withhold the tribute due the young lady.

"Then I'll be hanged if she isn't a phenomenon of goodness!" exclaimed the redcoat, his gaze following the object as she moved quietly out of their field of vision.

"Men like you and me, colonel, who have families of our own, cannot fail to be pleased when we have the privilege of meeting those whom we can hold up as models to our daughters."

The fine irony and rebuke contained in these

words, were lost upon the brutal Tory, whose eyes were still fixed upon the spot where he had last seen the object of his sudden admiration. He muttered, as if speaking to himself:

"I must see more of that beautiful young rebel!"

CHAPTER IX.

A QUARREL.

THE sudden turning of Colonel Denison's head, accompanied as it was by a peculiar expression of the speaker, while he was in conversation with the Tory Butler, was the first apprisal Rosa Minturn received that she was doing an imprudent thing in thus scrutinizing the leader of their enemies in so pointed a manner. Her face flushed crimson as she saw the eyes of Butler follow those of his informant, and she turned on her heel and lost no time in making herself invisible.

There is an instinct in woman that warns her of the approach of danger, and she felt as if she would give worlds had she refrained from attracting the attention of the Tory by her own actions. But, as that could not be recalled, she resolved, as the next best thing, to keep out of his sight altogether, refraining from showing herself, as much as possible, until after the departure of the invaders from the valley. This would have been no very difficult matter, provided she had not drawn the attention of the Tory to herself and awakened a determination on his own part to see her further, in short, to cultivate her acquaintance.

And so, as Rosa passed outside the fort, and sought to lose herself from the sight of her too ardent admirer, the latter did not wait long, but followed her. This was done in an apparently aimless manner; for Butler wished to make it appear that he was merely lounging about, with no other purpose than to watch the actions of those under his command. He was especially desirous of not alarming the object of his search by too great precipitancy. In fact, he acted, just as if he had gone out to show off his handsome form for her admiration, while he was not anxious to see any one himself. But there was an eager look in his face as he gazed around upon the motly swarm of people constantly coming and going.

"She does n't appear to be in sight," he muttered, after he had searched among the group for several minutes for the one who had so captivated him at first sight. "Denison tells me that she is modest, bashful, and all that sort of thing. Well, I'm sure I've no objection, for I'm blessed she is just the prettiest lot of homespun that I've seen for a long time. I wonder where on earth she could have

taken herself so quick. From the way she gaped
at me, there is no doubt she was impressed.
That's one reason why I take so much pains with
my uniform, for it's just the thing to catch the eye
of a young girl like her, even though it's getting
pretty well worn. There is something in a soldier,
especially if he is a brave officer, that they don't
seem able to resist. I am sure that it will be an
easy thing to win her love, and the taking of her
away as a prisoner will be still easier. A fellow
might as well enjoy himself in this world, and,
indeed, it becomes the duty of him to do all the
injury to the enemies of King George he can—
though I don't mean to harm a hair of her head.
Ah, no, the dear girl! But I was just thinking
that the old folks, as a matter of course, would
make a great fuss if their rosebud were plucked
by a British colonel and carried away, and
such a result, bringing distress, would be my
bounden duty to my king."

Colonel Butler was growing quite confidential
with himself; and as he stood staring round the
space before him, where the Tories, Indians and
patriots were passing to and fro, as if in review,
his gaze flitted here and there in his search for the

fair one, who seemed to grow more beautiful and attractive the longer she kept from his sight.

"Rosa Minturn, I am told, is her name. Well, that's pretty, but it can't be compared to her. Minturn, Minturn," he repeated to himself, musingly. "I know most of the families in the valley, but I don't recall him. Now, if that dog of a cousin of mine, Zeb, that fought us so hard hadn't slid out to Wilkesbarre, I could have found out all I wanted to from him, after which I would have had him shot as sure as I'm a living man, and I would have pleased my superiors by doing so, too."

When a man is very eager to meet some one, and is kept waiting, he is apt to lose his temper; and Colonel Butler, who was not possessed of an angelic disposition, was growing angry. For awhile he smothered his wrath for fear the beauty of his face might be marred when Rosa should catch the next view of it; but as this glimpse was a long time coming, he became so impatient that he was compelled to give expression to his feelings. This, as might be supposed, came at first in the shape of an imprecation, which all but himself and the recording angel failed to hear.

"It beats everything!" he added, "that all that I *don't* want to see are passing back and forth, and them that I *do* want to look upon ain't visible. I'll be hanged if I don't stand here all day, if it's necessary, to see her!"

The time was ill for any one to approach the colonel, but as it so happened, Colonel Denison, of all others, was the one who appeared at his elbow at this moment, and gently touched him.

"I am sorry to trouble you, Colonel Butler, but the Indians under your command are becoming worse every minute, and there is reason to fear that blood will soon be shed."

"What's the matter now?" growled the Tory leader, wheeling about and scowling at him.

"The Indians, who seem to belong to all the tribes of the Six Nations, are pillaging the houses of the settlers, and when I venture to remonstrate with them, they only grin in my face and appear to care nothing for my threat to complain to you."

"If they don't care for such a threat, what is the use of your coming to me with your whining, then?"

"To have it checked at once, as due to the

capitulation which you and I signed, and which has been fulfilled to the letter by me."

Angry as was the Tory, he saw it would not do to throw this appeal entirely aside, coming as it did from the officer with whom he had treated, and whose sword he had received.

"I'll see what can be done to stop it," replied Butler; "but the blood of the Indians is up, and there are so many of them that I don't believe they can be controlled."

"A colonel should never assume command of any body which he cannot control."

The Tory turned upon the patriot, his face working, for the rebuke was a cutting one, and all the more so from its unquestionable truth. The enraged Butler answered by assuring Denison he might go to the hottest place known, and then suddenly paused and glowered fiercely in his face, as if to hear what he was going to do about it.

There was but one course open for a gentleman. Colonel Denison was unarmed and on parole. Without a word he turned his back upon the conqueror of Wyoming, and walked away from him. Thus ended all intercourse between the two officers. Butler started after the patriot, as if he expected to see him turn and come back, but he was disappointed.

"I expected the Indians would kick up a muss about this time; it's the way they have of making war, and those who resist them must be prepared to pay the piper."

When a few minutes more had gone by he moved his position, concluding that it was best for Mohammed to go to the mountain, as there were no signs of the mountain calling upon him.

"The Iroquois may tomahawk every rebel in the valley—women, children and all—for ought I care, so long as they don't disturb any of the glossy tresses of my charmer."

An hour had passed since he had seen that wondrous face and form, and her continued absence led him to begin to suspect that perhaps, after all, there was a purpose in her remaining so long invisible.

"I don't know what it can be," he said to himself, as he reflected over the matter; "but whatever it is I will soon find out."

CHAPTER X.

RATHER TOO KIND.

COLONEL BUTLER carried out one of his threats, at least. Finding that the prospect of seeing Rosa Minturn was slight, so long as he held his first position, he changed it. But a mere change failing, also, to bring her to light, he resorted to inquiry or stratagem. The first point he played was to hunt up old Mr. Minturn, who was full of apprehensions of the trouble from the Indians. His house stood near the fort, and he was leaning on his cane in front of the building, with one or two of his neighbors, as if he were dubious whether it would do to attempt to occupy it for some time yet. They varied their occupation by stealing furtive glances at a group of Mohawks lounging about the settlement under the influence of liquor, and whom the patriots were anxious to avoid.

When the little party of white men saw the Tory colonel approaching, they saluted him, and Mr. Minturn ventured to ask whether the savages

might not be put under a stricter surveillance, so
that the danger could be nipped at the bud. The
reply of Butler was a signal to Minturn to come
to one side, so they could converse without being
overheard.

"You must have discovered," said he, in a confidential manner, "that there are more Indians than
white soldiers, and I see that they have managed
to get hold of some liquor somewhere; so there'll
be trouble. We shan't be able to control and keep
them down."

"Great heavens!" exclaimed the horrified old
man. "What is to become of us, then, if you can't
do anything with them? If you will give us our
arms back again, we'll take care of ourselves."

"That I would do if they were not already in
the hands of the Indians. However, there is no
reason for you to fear any harm to yourself and
family."

"Pardon me; but I fail to see why we are not in
as great peril as the rest of them."

"We shall be able to take care of some of the
rebels, and I promise you that I will see that no
harm comes to you and yours."

"I am sure I am deeply grateful for your kindness," replied the old gentleman, somewhat at a

loss to understand why it was he had been singled out for this mark of leniency. "But I wish you could extend your authority far enough to save all whose lives have been intrusted to your keeping."

"So do I; but as that is clearly impossible, I will do the next best thing—save all those whom I can. I understand that you have not been quite so outspoken in your denunciation of his majesty as many of your neighbors around you."

This was something after the order of the wolf and the lamb. The Tory felt that he must make some show of reason for the step he had decided to take, and he threw out this feeler, entertaining no doubt that the listener would greedily snap at it as a piece of diplomacy. But he underrated the sturdy patriotism of the old man, who answered, without a moment's hesitation:

"I cannot consent that you should grant indulgence or kindness under false pretenses on my part. I am sure that of all the settlers of the Wyoming valley there is not one who has been more bitter and severe than I in my denunciation of the brutal attempt of your king to subjugate the colonies of America. This much I must say in deference to truth itself. I cannot lie, even for the sake of saving my own life, and the lives of those who are dearer to me than all the world besides."

"At any rate," continued the Tory, with a lame effort to make his action appear consistent, "I understand that you have comported yourself more like a gentleman than the majority of your neighbors."

"That would be an arraignment of the motives of my friends, to which I cannot in justice submit, without protest. No, sir; you must class us all together in that respect."

Unable to explain satisfactorily what he had decided to do, the Tory had to resort to the only thing left at his command.

"Rest content with the assurance that I have the best of reasons for showing a more careful protection of the families of yourself and several of your neighbors. This is your house, I believe?"

"It is."

"Very well; how many members are there in your family?"

"I have a wife and daughter. My son is away."

"Where are the lady members?"

"I saw them a few minutes ago, but cannot say where they are just now."

"Hunt them up as soon as you can, and such others as you can accommodate comfortably in your residence. When you have done so, I will have a guard placed before the house and no one shall interfere with you."

"I am sure I am greatly obliged to you for your kindness, of which I shall avail myself without delay."

"Do so, and good-bye for the present."

And, saluting the little group, the members of which had been allowed to hear the last words, Colonel Butler withdrew. In the course of the next half hour, several families had installed themselves in the house of Mr. Minturn and among them were his wife and daughter. Later he received a call from no less a personage than Colonel Nathan Denison, the guard being in the act of assuming charge of the premises at that moment. After saluting the inmates, the colonel called Mr. Minturn aside and talked very earnestly with him. At the end of a few minutes he said:

"You may be safe here, but, if you will take the advice of a friend, you will not let your daughter Rosa stay until to-morrow."

"What shall I do?" asked the sorely troubled

old man, fully appreciating the warning he had received.

"Send her to Wilkesbarre to-night."

"But who will take her there?"

"I will find some one, and, if I fail to do so, I will escort her myself."

"Very well. It shall be done, if the thing is possible."

"Say nothing to anyone about it till the time arrives, which will be several hours after dusk."

The agreement having been made, Colonel Denison took his departure, little dreaming what was to come to pass before Rosa Minturn should be allowed to start on her flight through the wilderness to avoid the Tory colonel.

CHAPTER XI.

THE PLAN.

THE shades of night closed over Wyoming valley, and still no one knew of the intention of Lorimer Minturn, except himself and Colonel Denison. The good officer while carefully avoiding any direct contact with Colonel Butler, managed to keep his eye upon his movements and satisfied himself that the contemplated flight of Rosa Minturn was absolutely necessary for her safety. His knowledge of the unscrupulous Tory, aside from what he had witnessed during the day, convinced him that the man would not hesitate a moment to carry the girl back with him. But he believed that daring and nerve would speedily place her beyond her enemy's reach.

His great desire was to obtain the proper person to take charge of the undertaking; for, although ready to do it himself, he was sensible of his own disqualifications. There were plenty whom he could call to mind, but, unfortunately, they were not within reach. There was the old scout, Ike Wells, whom he had not seen for weeks past; but, superior to him, and indeed to all others, was the famous friendly Mohawk, Lena-Wingo, or Red Jack, as he was more generally known among the whites. This singular Indian had been one of the most devoted and faithful friends of the settlers for a half dozen years, and had performed deeds in their service almost incredible. Especially on the bloody field of Oriskany he had imperiled his life over and over again for the sake of the wretched fugitives, whose situation was fully as terrible as their fellow sufferers at Wyoming. But no one could tell where Red Jack was. There were rumors among the Tories and Indians that he had recently fallen by the hand of that dusky miscreant Brandt, but none of the patriots believed it. For all that, he had not been seen in the Wyoming valley for days, and so Colonel Denison dismissed him from his mind with a sigh of regret.

Next to these, in the estimation of the officer, came Ned Clinton and Jo Minturn, who, if the reports could be believed, were still prowling somewhere, keeping out of the way of the Indians and Tories. They were brave with a spirit of adventure, added to which was the fact that one was the brother and the other the warm friend of the young lady; so there could be no question about their readiness to engage in anything of the kind for her sake. But they, too, were absent, and were unlikely to return until the invaders should withdraw from the valley.

"So it looks as if I shall have to take charge of the business myself," said the colonel, as he revolved the matter in his mind for the twentieth time; "and if I do I'll go through with it, or somebody will get hurt. Colonel Butler hates me as bad as he does his own cousin, and he will go to any lengths to square accounts for my interference in an affair of his heart. If I wasn't actuated by a wish to befriend such a good girl as Rosa, whom I have known from her infancy, the prospect of checkmating such a scoundrel as he would be all the motive I could need."

It was certain that the Tory leader held not the remotest suspicion of the trick that was being arranged, for there was no reason that could possibly suggest itself to his mind. He still believed the young lady had been charmed by her first sight of him, and was only acting in accordance with the shy, coy disposition which he had been given to understand was a part of her nature. When she came to learn what extraordinary care he had taken to guard herself and family from disturbance, she would be filled with gratitude. It was more than likely that she would fall on her knees; or, what would be infinitely more agreeable to the old scamp, would throw her arms around his neck, and, with streaming eyes, call down the blessings of Heaven upon him for his noble generosity in her behalf. Nothing, therefore, was further from his thoughts than that this little bird-of-paradise would beat the bars of her cage, and, breaking out, fly away beyond his reach. Such being the case, the parties planning the piece of strategy were possessed of every opportunity they could ask, except the selection of the proper one to prosecute it through to the end.

Although Colonel Butler scowled upon Denison more than once when he saw him going to or returning from the house which was the great attraction to him, yet he was too politic to interfere, when it was plain the patriot was a particular friend of the family. The villain could afford to wait awhile before stepping in and spoiling that game.

The night was well advanced when Colonel Denison and the father of Rosa called her and her mother into an apartment where they were secure against interruption, and made known their whole plan, which could not but create dismay when first heard. The mother, more than the daughter, was disposed to oppose such a wild scheme as the departure of the child in the night, when it was necessary to cross the river and make a journey of several miles through the wilderness before they could reach a place of safety. But a few pointed words from Colonel Denison convinced both the ladies so thoroughly of the purposes of the Tory, that they were not only ready, but eager, that the imperiled one should be off.

"Having satisfied you of the necessity," said the colonel, with a quiet emphasis that could not be mistaken, "it only remains to agree upon the precise means."

"You will go with me?" said Rosa, with such an evident dread that the officer had arranged for her to make the journey alone that the others could not forbear a smile.

"I had strong hopes all day that I could find some one better qualified than I, but the very men whom I want, and to whom only I would entrust your escort—Red Jack, the Mohawk, old Ike Wells, and Ned Clinton and your brother Jo—are beyond reach, and so we'll have to get along without them. Consequently, I must elect myself commander-in-chief of the retreating party. Therefore, Rosa, if you will accept me as your escort, I will see you safely through, if the thing be among the possibilities."

"I would rather have you than any one in the world," replied the young lady, with the trusting simplicity of her nature.

Colonel Denison bowed gracefully in acknowledgment of the compliment to his friendship and honor, which was not misplaced.

"It is natural that you should look upon the venture with a little shrinking; but I have spent a good deal of time in thinking it over, and I cannot see that there is anything very formidable about it. We will cross the river within a mile from this point—"

"But *how?*" interrupted Rosa, who was naturally anxious to learn all about the expedition in which she was to play so important a part.

"I believe you are an excellent swimmer?"

"I have swam the Susquehanna, but I don't want to do it at night if it can be helped."

"Nor is it my intention that you shall. We shall have little trouble in finding a boat that will bear us safely—"

"Oh, yes," interrupted Rosa, again, in her impulsive way. "I know the exact spot where a canoe is drawn up in the bushes on the bank."

"And, if necessary, you can manage the paddle."

"Give me the chance, and I will show you."

"In short, I don't see why you are not fitted to make the journey without any companion at all. But that is all fixed, as I told you a minute ago. When across, we have less than five miles to travel, and as Rosa knows every foot of the way, we will reach Wilkesbarre before daylight."

"You are sure that Butler suspects nothing of this?" asked the father, in a low voice. "And none of the guards either?"

"It is impossible. Hello! What's that?"

At that moment there was a gentle knock at the door. As Colonel Denison sprang up and opened it, an Indian stood before them.

CHAPTER XII.

A VALUABLE ALLY.

THE consternation of the little group was overwhelming when the door was opened and they saw an Indian in his war-paint standing before them, his black, serpent-like eyes glittering as he looked down in the faces of the dismayed group.

All believed that this warrior was one of the guards, that had been set by Butler to spy out the doings of the conspirators, and who had been sent at this moment either to arrest or scatter them. For a few seconds not a word escaped any of the whites. They stared at each other, seemingly overcome to that extent that they could not command their utterance.

The Indian was very tall, and of thinner frame and more handsome features than are generally seen among his race. His face was so thickly covered with a compound of paint that, had he been an Adonis himself, he would have appeared frightful to the ordinary observer; but the patriots had long since become so accustomed to the most forbidding-looking creatures of his kind, that they were not impressed in this respect. The redskin was the first to break the silence.

"Am I welcome?"

The instant these words were spoken, in good English, and in a low, cautious voice, Colonel Denison gave a gasp of delight, and sprang toward the door.

"Give me your hand! Heaven itself has sent you, of all others, for I have been praying for your coming all day. Don't you recognize him, friends? This is Red Jack, our Mohawk scout, worth a dozen men at any time."

On being introduced in this fashion, the noted redskin grinned, showing a set of teeth as white, even and beautiful as those of Rosa Minturn. At the same time, he took a step forward, and softly closed the door behind him. Every white person present was acquainted with the famous Mohawk scout, and they instantly gathered about him, taking his hand, telling him, in cautiously modulated tones, of their pleasure at seeing him at this time.

He was a great favorite with Rosa herself, for whom he had shown an attachment from her earliest girlhood. He had taken her many a mile in his canoe, before the tide of war swept through the valley; he had shown her how to handle the long ashen paddle, and had taught her to fire the rifle with a skill scarcely second to that of the ordinary hunter. Rosa had accompanied the Mohawk many a time on long excursions into the forest, the confidence of all the settlers in the friendly Indian being perfect, as he had proven his loyalty on so many occasions and in so marked a manner that there could be no doubting it. Such being the case, it followed that Lena-Wingo, or Red Jack, was held in special abhorrence by the redskins of the Six Nations, or Iroquois, who were among the most faithful allies of the Tories, fighting in the interest of the sovereign of Great Britain. It was known that for years the Indians had been seeking the life of Red Jack, and Brandt had even offered a reward to any warrior who would bring him the scalp of the remarkable scout.

No one besides Red Jack himself could guess how often the attempts had been made against his life. Nor would it be safe to hazard a conjecture as to the number of times that, in the depths of the great wilderness, he had been attacked by some sinewy warrior ambitious of winning the distinction of killing so distinguished a character as the

renegade Mohawk, as he was called by his own
people and the white miscreants who had turned
against their own race.

After Red Jack had shaken the hands of his
friends over and over again, with his face on the
grin all the time, Colonel Denison asked:

"How did you manage to get inside, Jack?
Colonel Butler has a guard around the house, and
the Tories know you so well that I should have
been sure of their stopping you."

"Don't know Jack all the time," he answered,
signifying that he possessed more than one plan of
disguising his manner and appearance, so that his
worst enemy and best acquaintance could not
recognize him, particularly if he was favored with
the darkness of the night beside.

"I see," said the colonel—"I see, but where have
you been? We have had bad times in the
valley—"

"Jack know all about it," he interrupted. "See
Seneca Injun—he tell me."

"And you were missed, I can assure you."

"Didn't know Butler come here," said Jack, in
his quick, jerky fashion. "Jack was coming down
from Cherry valley—meet Seneca—he tell him all
about it—he hurry here."

This remark, it may as well be stated, strengthened a suspicion that Colonel Denison, in common
with others, held, to the effect that, although Red
Jack was practically outlawed by his race, yet he
had more than one friend among them, who
apprised him of many movements intended to
work him ill. But the officer was careful to keep
his suspicion from the Mohawk himself. Red
Jack made some inquiries of the whites as to the
fate of their friends—particularly of the two
young men, Ned Clinton and Jo Minturn—and he
was not a little pleased to be told that there was
every reason to believe they were out of danger.
Colonel Denison then proceeded to tell the scheme
for placing Rosa Minturn beyond the reach of the
Tory leader—the girl, of course, to be put in care
of the Mohawk. The latter stood in the middle
of the room, looking down into the face of the
colonel while he was unfolding the scheme. When
it was finished, he nodded his head to signify
that he understood what was expected of him.

"All right, all right; Jack will take her to
Wilkesbarre. He knows the way. He lead her
there to-night."

Rosa was the most delighted one of the party,
for, despite the enthusiasm with which she

received the announcement of the colonel that he was to be her escort, she was more pleased over the companionship of the Mohawk than she could be with any one else, for the reason that she knew that no five men were as competent as he. This was the whole thing in a nutshell, and so great was her trust in her dusky friend that she looked on the expedition much as she did upon her former excursions into the wilderness. The night was clear. There was a partial moon, and the air was just cool enough to make it pleasant without or within. So she was rather desirous of being under way.

The long slowly ticking clock in the corner showed that the fan-like hour hand was close on the figure eleven. It was time, therefore, that some move was made to carry out the programme, for at that season of the year the nights were short and the fugitives likely to need all the hours remaining to them. It was agreed, therefore, that in the course of the next ten or fifteen minutes the start should be made.

Red Jack, when he had the whole scheme of Colonel Denison, said that he would vary it considerably. Instead of crossing the Susquehanna at the point designated by the officer, he intended to keep on up the stream till he passed above "Queen Esther's Rock," as it has since been christened, for the reason that there was less likelihood of their attracting the notice of their enemies above than below the place named. After going over, he was inclined to favor a circuitous route instead of a direct one to Wilkesbarre, and he thought it likely that he would push back to the mountain range to the southeast, before making it.

It will be understood that the house of Mr. Minturn was simply guarded from disturbance from the outside, there being no intention of interfering with the freedom of the inmates. At the same time there was no restriction put upon the movements of those who desired to call at the house. The task which was projected was, therefore, so far as appearances went, quite simple in its character—about the only difficulty consisting in getting away without the departure being noticed. The faint moonlight, the presence of the two sentinels pacing up and down in front, and the single one keeping faithful ward at the rear of the premises, surrounded the work with some labor, but all were confident it could be accomplished with little danger.

Red Jack, having entered as a messenger from Colonel Butler to the owner of the place, it was advisable that he should pass out again in the same guise. The plan fixed upon, therefore, was for him to stalk boldly out of the front door and make his way to a well known oak, standing just outside the small cluster of settlements, and scarcely a couple of hundred yards from the fort itself, where he would await the coming of Rosa. When she should reach that point, the rest of the journey, to their minds, would be clear sailing.

Within five minutes of explanation of the whole plan the Mohawk passed out of the front door, with as proud a step as if he were the leader of the Iroquois himself, who had been holding an important council of war with his commander. He made his way to the appointed rendezvous, where he prepared to wait with the calm patience of his race, willing, if necessary, to stay there the night through, without the first twinge of dis- satisfaction at the delay of others. The plan of Rosa was simple, and, no doubt, the best one possible. She intended to throw her shawl over her shoulders and walk out of the front door just as the Mohawk had done, but to make her way with more caution to the old oak, taking care that she was not watched or followed by anyone. The stratagem to be employed by her was to imitate the gait of her mother so closely that it, together with her makeup, would lead any one to take her for her parent. It was characteristic of the affectionate and reverent nature of the girl that she should feel some repugnance against doing this, on the ground that it savored of something like burlesquing the gait of her mother, though, of course, her scruples were speedily overcome.

It was certainly strange how matters shaped themselves that night. Everything was in readiness when all were startled by a knock upon the outside door, the room in which they were sitting being separated from the main reception apartment.

"Stay where you are, and don't speak," said Mr. Minturn, rising to his feet, "and I will attend to the call. I don't understand who can want to see me at this late hour."

On repairing to the door and opening it, who should the old gentleman see before him but Colonel Butler himself?

"Good-evening," said the Tory, with a laugh, as he extended his hand. "I was going by when

I observed a light, and thought I would drop in and see how things are with you."

"Good-evening, Colonel Butler," said the host, speaking in a loud voice, so that those in the inner room might know who their unwelcome guest was. "It is rather late, but come inside."

With many apologies for disturbing the settler at this late hour, the Tory stepped within and took a seat. And there he sat for a full hour, till midnight came and passed, talking to the patriot, who was obliged to do his utmost to dissemble his impatience, while he answered his impertinent questions, as best he could, regarding his family, and more particularly about his daughter, his apparently trivial inquiries bearing an unusual significance in view of the incidents of the day. At last he rose to go, promising to do himself the honor of calling on Rosa the next day.

CHAPTER XIII.

THE FLIGHT.

THE first arrangement contemplated that Colonel Denison should act as the escort of Rosa Minturn until she was well by the fort, after which she could readily pass the intervening distance without any attendant. But, while Butler was in the adjoining room, this plan was changed. The patriot officer believed that the enemy was likely to hold the house under surveillance for an hour or two to come, on the principle of the smitten lover finding pleasure in looking upon the residence of her who holds possession of his heart.

No man is so foolish and "spooney" as the one who has no right to be so, and the colonel showed a commendable knowledge of human nature when he guarded against the too close attention of the individual whom they were seeking to avoid. Nothing would look more natural than to see the commander of the vanquished forces acting as the escort of the lady of the house, when going off on some errand, in the dead hour of the night.

But as the Tory, sooner or later, must discover
that the bird had flown, so he was almost sure to
find out the precise means by which it had been
done, and he would be the more convinced of the
plot if able to recall the fact that he had seen the
rebel colonel and her together on the night of the
disappearance.

Something less than a half hour after the departure of Butler, the lights in the house of the Min-
turns were extinguished, as if the inmates had
retired for the night. Within the next ten minutes
the figure of an old woman, as it appeared, came
out of the front door, and stooping, as if with old
age and weakness, began walking slowly in the
direction of the fort, the intention being to turn off
and pass behind it before approaching near enough
to attract the notice of any of the Tories and
Indians that seemed to be wandering everywhere,
despite the late hour of the night.

Rosa was so full of the scheme that she was in
danger of betraying her assumed character, by
returning to her natural elastic walk, but she tried
her best to keep in mind the parting instructions
of Colonel Denison, who, with her parents, were
watching her, as long as she continued visible,
from an upper window. She speedily disappeared

in the darkness, and those whom she had left behind could only pray for the success of the scheme, which had now progressed too far to be recalled.

When Rosa passed outside the gate, she almost ran against the sentinel who was pacing back and forth on his beat. So near was the collision, on account of the man turning at that moment, that she gave utterance to a slight exclamation of fear, upon which the sentinel raised his hat and apologized.

"Pardon my rudeness, miss. It was unintentional!"

The fact that he addressed her as a young lady alarmed Rosa, and led her to believe her folks were mistaken as to the flight not being suspected. But, without doing anything more than to bow, she resumed her walk, still stepping off far more actively in her excitement than was prudent or safe. Her heart throbbed violently, for the undertaking assumed a more formidable character than before, and the cries of marauding Indians—many of whom were at no great distance—caused her to shiver with terror and stare fearfully around, expecting to see the ones whom she dreaded as she did death itself.

She had reached a point midway between her
home and the rendezvous, when, to her dismay,
she caught sight of several straggling forms
almost directly before her, and only a rod or two
distant. She stopped in her rapid walk, uncertain
what she ought to do, for there seemed little choice
between going back and pressing forward. If the
men attempted to insult her, she could turn about
and flee to the protection of the sentinels in front
of her own door. But she wished to avoid this
return, if possible, for the reason that the night
was already so far advanced that time was becoming incalculably precious, and she believed that, if
she lingered much longer by the way, the whole
project must fail altogether.

While she stood wavering and undecided, the
moving figures seemed to swing off to one side and
out of her path. She instantly resumed her walk
in the direction of the oak, still timid, hesitating
and holding herself ready to turn about and flee
like a bird the instant the marauders ventured to
approach her. In the gloom of the night the fair
fugitive was unable to tell whether the dreaded
parties were Indians or Tories, and, in fact, it
made little difference to which race they belonged,
as one set was about as bad as the other.

Approaching a few steps nearer, she was able to make out that there were three of them, and they were white men, it following, of course, that they belonged to the Tory band of Colonel Butler, and they were as much to be dreaded as if they were so many Mohawks. Still further, they were under the influence of liquor to that extent that they were lolling against each other, and indulging in maudlin snatches of song. As yet they showed no signs of having seen the trembling girl, who was stealing along so timidly, and watching every movement on their part; but there was no telling when they would catch sight of her.

Under the circumstances, Rosa was well able to run a great deal faster than they, but in her not unnatural dread, she feared that they would fire their guns at her, or else call some one to their assistance and secure her capture before she could return to the protection of the guards she had left behind, or could reach the waiting Mohawk under the shadow of the oak. Urged onward by the knowledge that the night was fast wearing away, she crept still nearer them, who were staggering, first upon one side of the path and then upon the other, but, provokingly enough, refusing to leave it clear altogether for her to pass.

Finally it occurred to the fugitive that, by making a little detour, she could flank them without attracting their notice. With this purpose, she moved toward the left, and succeeded in reaching a point almost opposite, when they saw her.

"Hello!" muttered one of the trio, straightening up; "what have we here? It looks to me like some pretty young rebel."

There it was again; the men, drunk as they were, saw that she was not an old woman, as she had been trying to appear. As the words were uttered, the three took a step toward the object of their interest, showing that they meant to satisfy their curiosity as to the identity of the person who was abroad at this unseemly hour of the night. It was no time to play the part of the old lady, for if she ever needed all her nimble-footedness, this was the time and here was the place. Rosa did not pause to make reply, but, without appearing to run, she walked as rapidly as she could, as though from a natural hurry instead of fleeing from the party.

"Hold on there!" called out a second person, who was less under the influence of liquor than either of the others. "Hold on there, I say, young miss."

The only effect of this summons was to increase the speed of the girl, who was as terrified as it was possible for her to be and still retain her senses. The walk became a run, seeing which the three men immediately started in full chase after her.

"Just see her spin along!" exclaimed one of the pursuers, who was leading the others. "She goes like a deer. Stop, I say!" he added, in a still louder voice. "If you don't, I'll fire at you."

This was the last feather, and the frightened Rosa sped away with all the speed at her command. There was fleetness in such a gait, and she speedily left the Tories behind, seeing which, one of them attempted to fire his musket over the head of the fugitive, but missed striking her by a narrow chance.

Rosa was speeding in the direction of the tree, where she knew the Mohawk was awaiting her, and she was sure of making it in time, when, to her dismay, a fourth Tory suddenly appeared before her, directly in her path!

CHAPTER XIV

LENA-WINGO STEPS TO THE FRONT.

FOR one moment Rosa Minturn despaired, as the figure of the man appeared in the path before her.

"Have no fear, my dear Rosa; I will protect you from all harm."

It was the voice of Colonel Butler—the very man whom she was fleeing from. The knowledge gave her nerve again, and she rallied, and darting to one side, attempted to flank the man; but Butler had recognized her, and did not propose to let her slip through his grasp in this fashion.

"My dearest Rosa, I beseech you not to try to run away from a friend; it's I, Colonel Butler, the one that loves you more than all the world beside, and that you admire so much. Just put yourself in my care, and it will be all right."

But he was the one in whose care she did not mean to place herself, and she abated her exertions not in the slightest. It seemed, however, as if a fatality were following her, for just as she was sure of escaping him altogether, her foot tripped in something, and, although she did not fall, she saved herself so narrowly, that when she recovered, the Tory stood before her, with arms outspread, ready to enfold her within them the moment she took a step forward. It appeared useless to struggle any longer, and the poor girl paused, dismayed and despairing, neither advancing nor retiring.

"My darling, why so frightened, when I am here to protect you? Could you not know that I am ready to offer my life for you, even to save your ears from rude words?"

The gushing old zany had his arms outspread and was in the act of stepping forward, with the purpose of throwing them around the defenseless fugitive, when a dark form darted out from the shadow of the oak which stood near at hand, and sped with astonishing swiftness directly toward the Tory. The latter's ears caught not the step, which was like that of a shadow; but Rosa saw the figure and she recognized the Mohawk. Still she did not feel safe, as the discharge of the weapon and the shouts had created such an uproar and excitement, that a dozen men were hurrying toward the scene, and there were doubtless others who would appear in the succeeding few minutes. But when the Mohawk tried to travel he knew how to do it, and he was on his mettle just now.

Colonel Butler was in the middle of his gushing harangue, with his arms upraised and outspread, ready to clasp the beautiful figure before him, when one of his wrists was seized and he was whirled half way round as violently as if smitten by a cannon-ball, the spinning, top-like movement bringing him face to face with the Mohawk, whose painted countenance seemed to be a-gleam with the flame of passion.

"Let her be—go back—save yourself—'tis Lena-Wingo that speaks."

If these words needed any additional emphasis, they were given in the shape of a long knife that gleamed in the moonlight. One of the many curious and apparently contradictory characteristics of the famous friendly Mohawk was his repugnance to shedding the blood of his enemies. As a rule, a savage does not wait for the simplest kind of a pretext, but takes to murder as a duck to water; and when it is remembered that this warrior knew that hundreds were hunting him down as though he were a mad dog, this peculiarity is all the more remarkable. There were scores of Tories and redskins that had fallen by his hands, but in every case—with an occasional exception—it was a clear matter of self-defense on his part, where there seemed no other way of saving his own life. There were one or two instances where, under great provocation, he had restrained the strange impulse of mercy that seemed ever present with him, but of these we will speak at another time.

When Red Jack, or Lena-Wingo, went into the deadly business, however, there were no half-way measures about it. The scalp was bound to come, and there were wild stories told of the number of those ghastly trophies he had hid away some-where in the mountains. In the present instance he held Colonel Butler at his mercy, but he had not the remotest intention of hurting him.

The Tory knew the terrible redskin before he announced his name, and he was never more scared in all his life.

"Hello, Red Jack; is that you?" he asked in a quavering voice, that he meant to make appear cordial. "Somebody has alarmed the young lady, and I was about to protect her when you came up. Do you want to take her in charge?"

"I take her—you go." Then turning to the trembling Rosa, the Mohawk added, "Run yonder—don't wait."

The fugitive was on the point of making a start on her own account when this order was given. She therefore bounded off like a frightened fawn, urged on by the sight of the rapidly gathering reinforcements. The friendly Mohawk stood facing about so as to cover her flight, looking unflinchingly upon the whites and Indians who were hurrying to the spot. Colonel Butler, quick to discover that he was granted freedom of action, began edging away from the dangerous fellow at his elbow, feeling anything but safe so long as he was within striking distance.

It took but a few seconds, inasmuch as Lena-Wingo did not attempt to follow, he having no purpose of injuring him, as we have already shown. The moment the Tory colonel felt safe, and saw several of his own soldiers at his back, he called out, in the trumpet-tones of battle:

"Sieze him! Don't let him escape! It is Red Jack, the Mohawk! Ten pounds to the man who makes him a prisoner!"

Butler had two objects for the capture of the extraordinary Mohawk. In the first place, he was

wanted on general principles, for the great injury
he had done the royal cause, but it was plain that
he was in the act of taking away the "light of his
eyes" from Wyoming—and that was like death
itself, all of which will explain the excitement and
anxiety of the officer to prevent the red scout getting away at this time.

As he uttered his command, one or two took a
step toward the defiant Mohawk, who, with his
drawn knife and rifle, calmly awaited their coming.

"Lena-Wingo is alone," he said, noticing their
hesitation. "There are whites—there are red men
before me. Why do they not come and take me?"

This was a tantalizing threat, but it did not spur
the parties addressed, and Butler became furious.

"Are you all cowards!" he demanded, "that
you are afraid to seize a single man?"

The soldier standing next him was impudent
enough to say:

"If our colonel will lead us in the attack upon
the Old Scratch himself, we'll follow."

"But I have no arms!" fairly shouted the raging
officer, "or I would cut him down!"

The soldier had seized a sword, as he started to

rush to the spot, and he reached it to his commander. "Here you are!"

The weapon was thrust so unexpectedly into the hand of Butler that he was fairly caught, and, frightened as he was, he strode valiantly toward the defiant Indian, calling to his soldiers:

"Come on, you cowards, and I will show you your duty!"

Just then the Tory turned his head, expecting to see Lena-Wingo in full retreat, but, to his dismay, the Indian was actually stealing toward him, in a crouching position, as if tired of waiting for the combat to open.

It was more than Tory flesh and blood could stand, and Butler wheeled about, and stooping down, as if to avoid a descending blow, leaped back among his allies, several of whom indulged in a contemptuous laugh at the exhibition. At the same instant Lena-Wingo vanished.

"We'll have him yet!" exclaimed Butler. "He has started for Wilkesbarre with the lady, and he shall be headed off and shot before he can reach the place."

CHAPTER XV.

IN THE WILDERNESS.

WHEN the redskins saw that the famous scout had fled the fact gave them a courage which they had not felt up to that time. They were all adepts at trailing a foe, and they saw, as if by instinct, that the chance was in their favor for outwitting the dreaded scout. The latter was incumbered with the care of a young lady, which must necessarily impede his movements, and give them an opportunity to get in a treacherous shot when he was unprepared for it. This was a purely Indian business, and none but Indians took part in it.

Colonel Butler gave out that he would liberally reward the one who brought him the scalp of Lena-Wingo, or Red Jack, and he would double the amount provided the miss in his charge was also returned to him. Some six or eight redskins started in pursuit and the Tory awaited their return, impatient that he had been so stupid as to allow the bird to slip from his grasp.

If the great Mohawk scout was reckless in his bravery, he was also wonderfully skillful and shrewd with it all, and none knew better than he precisely what he was doing. He ran a hundred yards or more in his quick, noiseless way, until, having reached the point where he expected to find Rosa Minturn, he paused, and uttered a slight whistle.

He had hardly done so when his keen ear caught a rustling behind him, and he turned like a flash, ready for friend or foe.

"Is it you, Jack?" was asked in a soft whisper.

"It is Jack," was the answer, in the same guarded manner.

"I was afraid you were in trouble."

The Mohawk replied with a grin, invisible in the gloom.

"Are we ready to go on?" continued the fair fugitive.

"Yes, we go on. Follow me—keep close—do n't make noise."

Rosa walked as carefully as she could, but it was impossible to imitate her leader, who seemed to possess the power of making his way through the forest without a particle of noise. As he raised and put down his moccasin, the girl could not

detect the faintest possible rustle, nor was anything of the kind noticeable when he parted the
bushes in his path.

They were now in the wilderness, for the Wyoming valley, a century ago, might have been called
a wilderness as a whole, compared with its condition to-day.

The Mohawk knew he would be followed by half
a dozen of the most experienced and skillful warriors of his own tribe; but he cared nothing for
that. It would not be the first time, by long odds,
and he rather welcomed the thing, as likely to prevent the flight from becoming monotonous.

But the sly fellow said nothing of the kind to his
companion, for he did not think she was likely to
agree with him, and she might well question his
prudence. The only evidence that Jack gave of
fears of pursuit consisted in his occasionally stopping and standing as motionless as a rock, while
Rosa could barely make out in the night that his
face was turned, and he was looking over her head
back into the gloom, depending more upon his
wonderful power of hearing than anything else.

Rosa listened, too, as best she could, but the
silence of the tomb to her was not more profound.
A few minutes before, all was excitement and

uproar in the vicinity of the fort, but there was
nothing now to show that any one living person
was wi hin miles of where the two were standing.
The curdling sounds of rapine and murder—the
war-whoop of the redskins and the shouts of the
no less bloody Tories—these had died out for the
time, and were heard no more. But, for all that,
the minions of the night were abroad, stealing
like so many panthers approaching their prey.
They were groping here and there through the
wood, listening for some evidence of the precise
whereabouts of the Mohawk who had dared to
defy them to do their worst.

Every time the guide paused he raised his hand
as a warning to Rosa that she must not attempt
to speak, and she knew too much what the danger of disobeying the command might lead to, to
forget the warning. All the sound she heard was
the throbbing of her own heart, which she was sure
must attract the notice of Jack, standing at her
side, though he also refrained from opening his
mouth.

The second time they paused in this manner, the
silence to Rosa was as profound as at first, but the
action of the Mohawk showed he had detected
something suspicious; for he silently reached out

his hand and took hers, accompanying the movement with a soft "'Sh!" which checked the query that was already on her lips. Holding her hand in his own, he turned off at almost a right angle to the course they had been following up to that moment. The turn was to the right and was followed but a few seconds until it brought them to the edge of the river.

The broad Susquehanna was flowing calmly and smoothly in the faint moonlight, as though it had not witnessed the dreadful scenes that had taken place on its banks but a short time before. The stillness continued unbroken, but Jack was listening in the close, attentive way that showed he was expecting something. Nor was he disappointed; for within the next five minutes the sound of a paddle was heard so distinctly that his fair companion noticed it and turned to her guide as if to ask, by her manner, whether he had caught it.

There could be no failure on his part, and when she turned he repeated his "'Sh!" to prevent her speaking. At the same time he drew her back a few feet further from the water and placed himself between it and her. Both held these same positions for a few minutes longer, and then Rosa, who was listening and looking with all the ears and eyes she had, again caught the sound of a paddle in the water. Jack instantly recoiled, and extending his long, bony arm toward the river, whispered:

"Look."

Dimly visible was a canoe, in which several Indians were seated, while one of them plied the single paddle with such care that, had not the two been listening, they would have heard nothing of it. The meaning of the whole thing was so plain that Rosa read it without any help from her sagacious companion. Their pursuers, believing they were making for Wilkesbarre, had sent a number of scouts across to head them off, leaving, of course, enough on his side to prosecute the search unremittingly. The two stood and watched the boat with its suggestive occupants until it gradually faded out in the gloom of the night, when they relaxed their position of intense attention.

"Now we go up river," said he, breaking the quiet for the first time since starting fairly upon their flight.

"Where to?" she asked, glad, like all her sex, to avail herself of the chance to use her tongue.

"A little way," was the rather vague answer. "Tread light—walk still—make no noise—like Jack."

"I'll do my best, but I can't do as well as you, and you know it, Jack, and I don't believe any one else can do so either."

"Try."

They advanced with great caution, for there was every reason to believe a number of their enemies were close at hand, and a single inadvertence might betray them.

It was not the purpose of the Mohawk to cross the river for some time yet, and he cautiously pushed on, making unimportant progress until the gray light in the east told of the coming day. A halt was then made, and they waited where they were for all of an hour, when they pressed stealthily forward a short distance further. Before they could go beyond, they became the unwilling witnesses of a scene so appalling that even Lena-Wingo, the Mohawk, who had looked upon every imaginable atrocity, was shocked.

CHAPTER XVI.

QUEEN ESTHER.

The Mohawk and Rosa paused amid the dense undergrowth, and the red scout softly parted it in his front and peered through. The girl was several feet behind him and she did not dare to approach without permission, although her curiosity was great, for she was assured by his manner that he had discovered something of importance to both of them.

For the space of five minutes, perhaps, the Indian did not stir a muscle; but, during this time, the girl heard sounds beyond them. There were confused voices,—those, no doubt, of their enemies,—and some sort of a busy scene was going on directly before the eyes of the watcher. By and by Lena-Wingo turned his head, so that he faced the girl who was watching him so closely, and silently beckoned to her. Rosa was at his side next minute, crouching like one who knew the need of the utmost caution.

"Make no noise," whispered her friend. "Watch much—won't hurt."

The scene that Rosa gazed upon she remembered to her dying day. If Lena-Wingo could have comprehended the sensations that were produced upon the fair fugitive by the sight, he would never have permitted it; but he was an Indian, and could not be expected to comprehend such things.

On the brow of a high steep bank, which, no doubt was the ancient shore of the Susquehanna, is a boulder, rising about a foot and a half from the ground. It is a sort of conglomerate, composed principally of quartz, and is still an object of great interest to tourists. Gathered around this rock were sixteen white men, who had been taken prisoners at the battle of Wyoming and were doomed to die by the hand of a single woman. This woman was Catherine Montour, better known, perhaps, as Queen Esther, for whom the rock referred to is named.

This extraordinary creature was a half breed who had been well educated in Canada, and she was a favorite with the best society in Philadelphia before the Revolution. And yet, in that fair bosom beat a heart as fiendish as that of any of the Tories or redskins. She followed in the train of the invading army that entered Wyoming, and committed atrocities that are incredible. These were mainly done, it is said, in revenge for the loss of a son who was shot by a scouting party a few days before. But there are other well established tales of this Hecate, which can be explained on no other ground than absolute fiend-ishness of heart, that found its supremest delight in witnessing the torture of a fellow creature, if she could only be sure that in his veins flowed the blood such as was partly in her own.

Queen Esther, by virtue of her office among the Iroquois, where she was looked upon as a verita-ble queen,—she occupying a palace, as it was called, at the head of Seneca lake, where the town itself was named Catherine in her honor,— assumed the office of executioner. The sixteen white men who had been taken at the massacre were arranged around this rock. They were all placed under the charge of a strong guard of Indians, whose business it was to place the victims in position to receive the finishing stroke from the feminine fury. At the moment Rosa Minturn gazed out from her hiding place beside the friendly Mohawk, three men had already fallen by the death maul and hatchet of Queen Esther.

The sixteen prisoners were first stood up in a row, within a rod or so from the boulder, which they faced, so that they saw all that passed. When the queen was ready, the first man was led forward, and seated on the rock, still guarded by a strong force of Indians, who were guarding against any attempt to escape. The woman, as soon as the victim was ready, took her station directly in front, and, chanting a low monotone that sounded like the humming of the gale through the cordage of a vessel at sea, she sank the hatchet, with one sweep, in the brain of the man before her, chanting her dirge, or death-song the while.

The whites seemed stupefied and helpless as by a spell of horror, which rendered them incapable of resistance. When one of them was conducted forward, he walked as meekly as a lamb, and sat down, never stirring after the warrior stepped back so as to allow the queen the room she wanted. Sometimes the white man looked up into the face of his executioner without raising his unbound hands; sometimes he made an instinctive attempt to ward off the blow. Again, if the victim happened to be gazing downward at the time he was placed in position, he generally continued in that posture until the fatal blow had descended. One sweep of that swift arm was generally sufficient, the keen edged tomahawk sinking into the skull as if driven into the yielding earth itself. As soon as the blow was given, the man, as a rule, sagged heavily downward and rolled off the rock, and was dragged out of the way to make room for the next victim.

The first glance that Rosa Minturn obtained of this scene showed that three victims had already fallen and that the fourth was being led forward. The girl recognized him as one of her nearest neighbors, and there was a certain bravery and stoicism in the action of the man that at any other time would have won the admiration of the Indians themselves. The two who had him in charge stopped at his side as if they intended to hold him in place; but his lips were seen to move as if he said something, probably of protest, that they seemed to understand. They looked into each other's faces, as if consulting, and then stepped back and left him alone upon the rock, with the avenging fury standing before him, tomahawk in hand, waiting until all was ready before she struck the blow.

There was no shrinking or trembling there. The patriot stretched out his legs as coolly as if seated in the old tavern at Stroudsburg, and threw one foot over the other, just as if he were composing himself to tell some story to a crowd of gossips. Then he folded his arms in the same deliberate fashion and turned his head to one side and looked up into the face of the Indian queen, as if to ask why she was delaying the funeral. His lips were seen to move again by the watchers, although it was impossible for them to hear what the words were. The queen heard them, however, and paused a moment in the dismal chanting of her dirge, looking down at the face turned unflinchingly up to her own. For one second this tableau impressed itself upon the vision of the observers. The dozen men standing in a row, stolid, despairing and woe-smitten, guarded by twice as many armed Indians; the painted warriors gathered around and looking upon the execution; the victim seated on the broad rock; the Indian queen standing directly in front, with uplifted hatchet, poised and ready to strike—all this formed a picture which no person, fortunately, is called upon to view twice in a lifetime. But it lasted only a moment. The

THE INDIAN QUEEN STANDING DIRECTLY IN FRONT, WITH UPLIFTED HATCHET.—Page 128.

death-song that had been suspended for the instant, was resumed. The upraised tomahawk was seen to flash for a second as it was whirled over the head of the raging fury, and good, honest, brave Elijah Hapegood, rolled over and off the stone, his skull cloven in twain.

CHAPTER XVII.

A STRUGGLE FOR LIFE.

Thus the awful tragedy went on until eleven men had fallen before the hatchet of Esther, Queen of the Iroquois. The twelfth man was one named Hammond, who was placed upon the rock to receive his death blow.

Among the very few awaiting their turn was a brother of this victim, named Lebbeus, who was standing near a friend named Joseph Elliott, the two being noted for their great fleetness of foot. Every eye was fixed upon the scene, the Indian jailers apprehending no attempt to get away, as the tragedy was nearly over and no effort at escape had been made as yet. When Hammond saw his brother placed upon the rock, and the savage queen preparing to strike the blow, he said in a low voice to Elliott, who was standing close by his side:

"Let's try it."

"All right! Go ahead!"

Both bounded away at the same instant, the suddenness of the movement freeing them from their captors without a struggle. It was the belief of both the fugitives that they would be shot dead while running, and they preferred such a death to that which their companions had suffered, or were doomed still to suffer. But the desperate bound that they made was so unexpected to the Indians, that, for the few succeeding minutes—valuable beyond price to Hammond and Elliott—no gun was fired, the redskins simply trusting to their legs to overtake the fleeing whites.

Hammond was greatly surprised that no shot was sent after them, but concluded that the Indians believed in their own superior fleetness so well that they did not think there was any doubt of the recapture of the fugitives. The latter had run but a short distance when they were wise enough to separate, there being a better chance in doing this than in staying together.

Both ran like deer, and the pursuers did not seem to notice that they were gradually veering away from each other. Hammond headed up-stream, but had run only a short distance when he looked over his shoulder and saw the redskins were shaping their course with the expectation of shutting off the fugitives before they could reach Forty Fort. This was favorable, as it showed that the Indians, discovering the fleetness of the two white men, had thrown up the direct pursuit, and, feeling certain that the fugitives were aiming to make the fort, the redskins started to "cut across lots," and capture them in that way.

The instant Hammond detected their plan he headed still more directly up-stream, and, spurred on by the belief that there was a chance for life, exerted himself to the utmost, and ran with astonishing swiftness. While going at this furious gait, his toe caught in a vine, and he went forward on his hands; and so great was his speed, that he rolled over and over before he could check himself. When at last he did come to a full stop, he found he had been plunged, head first, into the dense top of a fallen tree, where he was so well hidden that he concluded to stay there, for the time being at least.

He had lain but a few minutes, when the Indians who had run to head off the return to the fort missed the fugitives and entered the woods to look for them. Hammond heard their stealthy footsteps near him and he was in despair. His violent exercise caused such a beating of the heart and hastening of the breath, that he was sure he would be betrayed by that means. No one can imagine his feelings as he detected the soft tread of the moccasins passing near him, and now and then caught a glimpse of forms through the interstices of the leaves. To top it all, one of the Indians actually drew the bushes aside almost directly over his head, but the twilight that reigned in such dense shadow prevented the fugitive being seen, and a moment afterward he went away.

Hammond did not dare to stir from his hiding-place until all was still. Then he stole cautiously out and made his way to the river, which he swam to Monacacy island, where he paused to rest a few minutes, but he was afraid to remain there, as he knew it had been used already to such an extent by the fugitives that he would not be safe. Accordingly, he entered the water again, with great care, and swam to the other shore. There he felt quite secure, but he continued his flight until he reached Wilkesbarre, where he was safe against further molestation from his vengeful enemies.

Matters had been more lively, if possible, with Elliott, who made his daring attempt to escape at

the same time. The latter was fully as fleet of foot
as his friend, and, like him, discovered that the
redskins were seeking to cut off his return to Forty
Fort. He, too, shaped his course for the river,
aiming, however, for a point so far removed from
the destination of Hammond that they failed to
see each other while pursuing their flight.

When Elliott struck the Susquehanna, it was
below Monacacy, and he swam out to the bar on
the lower portion. It was his purpose, as the distance was quite short, and he was an excellent
swimmer, to make the whole way under the surface, and when he calculated that he had
gone far enough, he came up, with his head well
out, but found he was still considerably short.
The Indians had not lost sight of him either, as he
discovered the next minute, when the sharp crack
of several rifles sounded on his ear, and a twinge
in the shoulder made him aware that he was
wounded.

For a minute or two he believed it was all up
with him, and that he was doomed to die; but the
recollection of the scene from which he had fled
nerved him to another desperate effort, and, by an
almost superhuman endurance, he succeeded in

reaching the eastern shore, with the width of the Susquehanna between him and his enemies for the time. Elliott deserved good fortune for what he had attempted, and it came to him. While he was wondering how he was to get along with his painful and bleeding shoulder, he discovered a horse quietly grazing near at hand.

"Thank heaven!" he exclaimed. "If I can catch him, I am saved!"

The animal showed no fear when he approached it, and in a few minutes he had his hand upon his mane. But there was neither bridle nor saddle, and he could not get along very well without the former, with which to guide the steed. As the best thing that could be done, he stripped the bark from a hickory-sapling, and from this made a rein that answered very well. The absence of the saddle was a small matter, and once upon the back of the beast, he headed him toward Wilkesbarre, and compelled him to do his best.

The fort was reached in safety, and a short while afterward Hammond came in and greeted him. The surgeon at the fort dressed the wounded shoulder, and the next morning Elliott made his way to Catawissa, with his wife and child, in a canoe, managed by a lad. There he was well taken care of, and he and Hammond lived many years afterward to tell their children of their wonderful escape from the fury of Queen Esther.*

---

*The incident described above is simply a fact and nothing more. The two men there named—Lebbeus Hammond and Joseph Elliott—as is stated, lived a number of years after. There is a possible variation in the exact *time* of the incident, as given by the writer.

CHAPTER XVIII.

A LABYRINTH OF PERIL.

WHAT more dreadful scene for man or woman to look upon than the one we have attempted to describe? Poor Rosa Minturn was held to the spot, transfixed by a strange fascination that comes over the strongest man, when confronted by some dread for which he has had no time to make preparation. Even the iron-hearted Mohawk, Lena-Wingo, who had looked upon and faced by himself all the known barbarities 'of war, was scarcely less impressed by the sight of Queen Esther's fury, and he neither moved nor spoke for several minutes.

Strangely enough, it was Rosa herself who first recovered from the stupefying spell that held her faculties bound for the time. With a mournful sigh, like that of the victim who manages to shake off the subtle power the rattle-snake sometimes weaves around him, she rallied, and comprehended her situation. What was to prevent some of those Indians from coming in the direc-

tion where she and her guide were so imperfectly
concealed? And what possible escape could
there be, in such an event, from the fury of the
Hecate?

Such were the questions that the brave girl put
to herself, and she knew, too, that nothing could
please Catharine Montour and her red allies more
than to cause these two fugitives to take the place
of the couple that had fled. But whether such was
the fact or not, she felt that she could no longer
gaze upon the shocking scene. At the risk, therefore, of offending Lena-Wingo, she reached out
her hand and gently touched his arm. He started
and looked into her pale face.

"Come," said she in a whisper; "don't let us
stay here any longer!"

"No, no," he answered in a strange, startled
way; "'tis bad—make girl feel bad—Lena-Wingo
bad man—bring you here—he sorry—we go way
—'Sh!—make no noise."

The two were themselves again, and they began
their retrograde movement in the same stealthy
manner that they had advanced to the spot. The
confusion resulting from the flight of Hammond
and Elliott was at its height just then, and as the
greater part of the Indians had dashed off in

pursuit, there was danger that some of them might come upon these two, who were striving so carefully to leave the perilous neighborhood.

None could know this better than the Mohawk himself, and he threaded his way with as much pains and stealth as if he were entering a camp of his enemies who were watching for his coming. He kept his fair companion as close to him as possible, and at every step or two he paused, and looked around, showing by his manner that he felt the danger was as likely to come from one direction as another. Nor was a whit of this extraordinary precaution thrown away. Indeed, nothing else could have saved them; for, without intending to do so, the Mohawk had led his gentle friend into a labyrinth of peril which he regretted on her account.

They had advanced less than a hundred feet from the last starting point, and the guide had paused again, as was his practice, when his keen ear detected the approach of something before Rosa herself could know it. With his warning "'Sh!" he stooped down as low as possible, and looked around with a slight nod of his head for her to do the same. The girl did so on the instant, and the cracking of a twig at that moment told her the meaning of the precaution. She glanced toward the point from which came the suspicious sound, and seeing nothing, looked again at the Mohawk.

He had gathered his feet under him, so that, if necessary, he could make a bound, without rising to a standing posture, and his hand rested on his knife in a way that was suggestive. The Indian was at bay, and he was as cool, too, as if seated by his own camp-fire in the depths of the forest. There was a peculiar gleam in his black eye, and he looked very much like a man whom it would be dangerous to disturb. But the stealthy footstep drew steadily nearer and nearer, until discovery was inevitable.

The sound showed that the enemy was closer to Rosa than to Lena-Wingo. Unpleasant as was this discovery, the girl did not dare to change her position, as the slightest movement was likely to betray them. But, if she was aware of the proximity of her enemy, so was her companion, who was there to protect her, and he was ready to do it with his life, at all times. He had his keen eye upon the point from which came the gentle rustling, and he was not to be taken off his guard.

Rosa Minturn was gazing in her fixed manner, when she caught sight of an object, the meaning of which she did not understand. It was on the ground, among the leaves, and not more than ten feet from where she was crouching in terror from the Indian drawing steadily nearer each second. Her first supposition was that it was the head of some serpent gliding over the leaves; and as it was coming toward her, she turned to Lena-Wingo and silently pointed at it, as if to ask him what should be done. The Mohawk nodded his head, but did not open his lips. He meant to say that he saw it, and would attend to whatever it might do.

When he nodded his head, he supposed that it was also understood by the young girl, though it was not. The object, as it appeared to her, was composed of several sharp glittering points that sparkled in the dim light of the shade as if they were jewels, or, what seemed more likely, the eyes of some kind of reptile. The thing—whatever it was—whisked into view, remained silent a minute, and then vanished, only to reappear as abruptly as before. When it came in sight the last time it was closer than before, and was so distinctly shown that the frightened girl recognized it.

It was the fore-part of an Indian moccasin! The action of the foot-gear proved still further

that it covered the pedal extremity of a warrior,
who was picking his way with such extreme care
as to show that he knew he was almost in the
presence of some enemy. Most probably, he
thought he had come, or, rather, was coming,
upon the lurking-place of one of the fugitives that
had made the desperate flight from the bloody
rock of Queen Esther. He was, therefore, moving
here and there, until he could determine the precise point where the patriot was in hiding, naturally seeking, at the same time, to keep his own
movements from the knowledge of the fugitive
himself. Screening his body in this careful manner, he exposed a few inches of his moccasin, without knowing that by that means he revealed his
position as well to the watchful Lena-Wingo as if
there were no intervening bushes to hide the rest
of his person from view.

For perhaps a dozen seconds, nothing but this
tell-tale motion of the beaded work showed itself.
The Indian was using eyes and ears, looking
here and there with the sharpness of a veteran of
the woods, while he listened intently that the falling of a leaf would have been heard by him. But
nothing was seen or heard by the enemy that could
add anything to what he already knew. It was

necessary, therefore, that he should make another slight change of position. Without stirring either foot, he bent his body forward, and pulled the bushes apart.

Rosa Minturn, happening to turn her head at the same moment, warned by a subtle instinct of danger, saw the painted face of a Seneca warrior within arm's length of her own.

CHAPTER XIX.

AN ENEMY AND YET A FRIEND.

THE sight of the painted countenance of a Seneca warrior, suddenly thrust through the parted
bushes within a foot or two of her fair face, was
a shock to Rosa Minturn, but she did not scream
or make any outcry that might have revealed their
situation to other enemies who were within a
short distance. With a slight gasp that could not
have been heard more than a rod away, she placed
her hands over her face and threw her head forward toward Lena-Wingo, appealing to him to
save her from the fury of the redskin who had discovered her. She was sure that the next minute
the two Indians would be closed in deadly encounter; but, to her amazement, several seconds
passed. During that time—seemingly much longer
than it really was—neither the Mohawk nor the
Seneca stirred a muscle! When the suspense
became unbearable, Rosa turned her head to learn
what it all meant.

A strange spectacle met her eye. The two red-skins, representing the extreme of sentiment among their own race, were looking in each other's face, and making some sort of signs with their fingers. And, furthermore, the first glance of Rosa told her the astonishing fact that there was no anger in the eyes that encountered each other in the wood on that summer morning. No; Lena-Wingo, representing the white race, as may be said, and the Seneca, fresh from the scene of one of the most inhuman massacres of the patriots, with his passions inflamed by what he witnessed and at which he helped, were face to face. It would naturally be supposed that the deadliest kind of a fight would instantly follow, but they were as gentle as two cooing doves.

We have said in another place that Lena-Wingo had his friends among his own race—warriors who would befriend him stealthily—scarcely aware that there were any except themselves so disposed toward him. These redskins would assist him when it could be done without risk to themselves, but in the presence of others there were no more savage foes than they.

When Rosa raised her head the Seneca seemed to feel that he was running more risk than was

10

prudent by allowing his countenance to be seen
at such a time by a third party, who might have
some future chance of giving evidence against
him. Accordingly, he withdrew his face, vanishing
so suddenly, and apparently in such trepidation,
that to any one who understood the situation
the scene could not but be amusing.

Rosa was quick-witted enough to understand
the simple fact that the strange Indian had played
the part of a friend, even if she failed to comprehend the precise reason why he did so; and something in the manner of the Mohawk told her
further that he sympathized with the dread of the
Seneca. The girl, therefore, said nothing, acting as
if she supposed that the redskin had withdrawn
from their presence through personal fear of a collision with the dreaded Red Jack, or Lena-Wingo.
But, if such were the fact, the first thing the
Mohawk would have done, after getting the
opportunity, would have been to change his
quarters, so as to prevent his enemy coming back
with reinforcements. Instead of that, the scout
showed a disposition to stay where he was for a
time longer, at least, for several of the Indians
that were looking for Elliott and Hammond were
so near that it would have been about impossible

for the fugitives to move without betraying themselves.

The strange forbearance or friendship of the
Seneca did not end with his simple retreat, after
discovering the hiding-place of Rosa and her guide,
as the latter knew it would not, but it was shown
in the most effective way. The Seneca was less
than a dozen yards from where he left the two in
hiding, when he met a couple of warriors stealing
toward the same spot, confident of finding one of
the fugitives that had made the dash for freedom.
It was only the work of a moment for the Seneca
to explain that he had "bored out that well,"
and it was no use of digging there for anything
in their line. And so the Indian turned away, and
with him went two others that were drifting in
that direction.

This general turning back caused a change in the
line of the search of a portion of the party for the
runaway fugitives, and possibly contributed in
this indirect manner to their ultimate escape.
Lena-Wingo was not slow to comprehend the
situation and he resumed his flight, prosecuting it
in the same careful manner as at first. The longer
this retrograde movement continued, the more
secure did he feel that he and his charge were safe

from disturbance. By signs that were unmistakable to him, he knew that the search for Hammond and Elliott had taken another course from that which placed Rosa Minturn in such peril for a time, and so he was left free to prosecute his way in his own peculiar fashion.

There was one fact that did not escape the sagacious Lena-Wingo at this time. During all the flurry, resulting from the flight of the two men, while the redskins were darting and stealing here and there through the woods and undergrowth, the Mohawk had not seen a single redskin that had started from Forty Fort the night before, by orders of Colonel Butler, to capture him and Rosa Minturn. It will be remembered that the two had watched a canoe crossing the Susquehanna a short time after the flight began, but the pursuers were not foolish enough to send all the force detailed for this special work in one direction, on the grounds that it was probable that the fugitives had gone that way. Some of them must still be on the west side of the Susquehanna. What, therefore, was the meaning of their failure to show up when in the vicinity of the massacre by Queen Esther?

Where the forest was tramped in all directions by such a number of fleeing men and their pursuers, anything like a systematic trailing of the Mohawk and the maiden was out of the question. The conclusion that Lena-Wingo educed from this fact was that, although a few of his own followers were on his side of the river, yet they had become convinced that the parties they were hunting had either crossed the stream or were making ready to do so, and consequently they were watching for them at the river side.

There were two courses of action left open for him. The first was to keep on up the left bank of the Susquehanna until a point was reached where it could be passed without much danger of discovery, and the other was to ascend far enough to feel pretty sure of keeping out of the way of any skulking redskins, and then to cross at night. There was not much choice between these two horns of the dilemma, for both rendered it impossible to reach Wilkesbarre before night should come again, and there was little difference in the danger attending each.

Lena-Wingo had a habit of thinking and deciding quickly upon a course of action, and it did not take more than a minute or so for him to

make up his mind to remain on the left bank until
night. He foresaw that the real difficulty still
was before him, for the Indians who had gone
over to intercept his flight to Wilkesbarre would
guard the approaches thereto with all the skill at
their command. They would discover in some
way that he had not reached his destination, and
scattering through the woods which surrounded
the station at that day on all sides excepting the
river, would leave no means untried to prevent
his doing so. But this was the sort of work
to which he had been accustomed for years,
and it had not lost its attraction.

However, he felt the responsibility of the care of
the fair girl, whose life had been intrusted to him,
and this rendered him more anxious than could
have been the case under other circumstances.
But, having decided upon his course, it was necessary that he should attend to another duty.

CHAPTER XX

THE OTHER DUTY.

LEXA-WINGO quickly explained the additional duty that claimed his attention. As they were to spend another day as fugitives, it was necessary that something in the way of food should be secured, with which to prepare themselves for the work before them. Rosa protested that the difficulty was too great to be encountered, and was sure that she could get along without anything to eat. Had the Mohawk been alone, he would not have thought the matter worth a thought. He had gone for days, when upon the warpath or trail, without a mouthful. But he knew how the case stood with his fair companion, and he answered her protests with the declaration:

"Must have eat—girl get weak—can't run—can't row boat."

All through the Wyoming valley, more than a score of miles in length, were scattered the dwellings of settlers, but it was not to be expected that any of the owners were at home. Those who had not taken refuge at Forty Fort had fled to Wilkes-barre, or some other place of safety. In most instances, nothing of their stock was to be found. At such a time, too, it would have been useless to hunt for game, and the maiden was justified, there-fore, in looking upon the attempt to procure the food as one not only of great difficulty, but of equally great danger. But there was nothing to be gained by attempting to combat the Mohawk when he once decided upon his course.

The movements of the two for an hour had resulted in placing them so far outside of the rov-ing bands of pursuers that they possessed some-thing like freedom of action. Lena-Wingo stepped off more rapidly, and with a greater swiftness and confidence than before. He went along with his old loping stride, which cost his fair companion quite an effort to equal. As they progressed they partly left the woods, frequently coming out into the open, cleared spaces, where they were naturally exposed to the view of any who might be in the vicinity.

At such times, Rosa was a prey to a dread which she could not conceal. It seemed to her that noth-ing was more natural than that some of their enemies were lurking in the neighborhood, in which event it was the easiest thing in the world for them to pick off both her and her companion by means of a stealthy rifle shot. She strove to convince herself that Lena-Wingo would not run such a risk when he had her under his protection, but the knowledge of the daring, reckless nature of the man shut off much comfort from that source.

This kind of progress was kept up for a considerable time longer, when they paused near a small house that had evidently belonged to one of the humblest settlers in the valley. The building itself was quite small, with a still smaller barn attached, but there were signs of thrift visible all around, several acres being under cultivation, while the garden belonging to the house showed plainly that a neat and industrious housewife had once presided there. But the occupants were gone— whether massacred or whether they had fled could only be conjectured. Be that as it may, another thing was also patent—all their live-stock was gone as well.

If the owner, learning of the storm that was approaching, had hied away to quarters which he considered safer than the fort, further down the valley, he had been deliberate enough in what he did to drive off his animals with him. And yet Lena-Wingo showed by his actions that he counted upon obtaining something there in the way of food, for he made the first halt since starting on the search proper.

"Do you expect to find something to eat?" asked Rosa.

"Eat there," was the answer.

"But it may contain Indians or Tories, Jack," she replied, glad of the chance to put in a disclaimer against his headlong manner of managing his business.

"You stay here—wait, watch. Lena-Wingo go see if Injun there."

As both were at that moment standing in an open space, where they were peculiarly exposed to the view of any one approaching or going away from the building, to say nothing of any who might be hiding within, it struck the girl as anything but a brilliant piece of strategy; but before she could protest, he motioned her to follow him to a small clump of trees near at hand, where something like concealment could be obtained. There she felt more secure, and promised to stay where he left her, and to keep the best watch possible.

The Mohawk did not wait a moment after giving her this direction, but started straight for the house, which was about a hundred yards away, walking with his long, loping stride, such as he used when he felt that the way before him was comparatively free from danger.

"He is so reckless that he is sure to get into trouble," muttered Rosa, as she watched him from her partial concealment.

The next instant Lena-Wingo reached the humble structure, which was two stories in height, with two windows on the side toward her. Her heart throbbed when she saw him enter the door, and she felt that the critical moment had come for her as well as for him.

If she was filled with fear and apprehension when he vanished in the house, what were her feelings when she saw the very next minute the figure of a redskin at the upper window? Yet there was no mistake about it. The sash was raised, for the weather was midsummer, as will be remembered. The redskin not only appeared at the opening, but he stopped and looked out.

"He is lost!" she thought. "Why was he not more careful? All is lost!"

To her horror, the Indian the next instant showed by his action that he was looking in the direction where she was standing. Still worse, he was actually making signals that must be meant for her. What should she do? If he had seen her —and he assuredly had—there was no means of escape, for, as close as was the wood, the fleet-footed savage could readily overtake her before she could go far.

"What can he mean by beckoning to me?" the affrighted maiden asked herself, sorely puzzled indeed.

"Oh, *now* I understand!"

A moment later she was laughing at her former fears; for she recognized the redskin as no other than Lena-Wingo, who was doing his utmost to tell her the way was open and she might approach with safety. After such notice it need not be said she did not let the grass grow under her feet.

It was strange that now, when her great fear was removed, that she became sensible of the fact that she was in need of food, and felt like commending the prudence of her guide in stopping for that purpose.

The Mohawk was at the door to meet her, and lost no time in explaining that the dwelling was

not only free from their enemies, but he had found
enough food to afford a substantial meal. He
proved the truth of this by producing a whole loaf
of bread, that was left in the pantry by the owner
in his flight, but the most thorough search failed
to discover anything else. But the maiden was
thankful to have even that, and the two seated
themselves and completed their strange meal.

The Mohawk was in excellent spirits, in spite of
the fearful scene they had witnessed only a short
time before, and he indulged in some facetious
observations that brought a smile to the face of
Rosa more than once, despite herself. But she
could not shake off a haunting fear that came
again and again, and, when the dinner was
finished, found expression:

"Jack, suppose some of them should come and
and find us here?"

"Injun won't come. Eat all want. We all alone
here—"

The broken sentence was not yet completed when
the speaker stopped short in his utterance. Well
he might. For at that moment they heard, beyond
a doubt, the sound of their enemies approaching
the house, and they were close at hand, too.

CHAPTER XXI.

A STRANGE ESCAPE.

NEVER did the Mohawk show his wonderful self possession and marvelous resources to better advantage than when he made the discovery that a party of the Indians whom he was seeking to avoid were approaching the house in which he and Rosa Minturn were seated, and were already so close that it was impossible to escape by flight No man is so wise that he does not at times make some mistake, and the Mohawk, although keen above his kind, had committed an error that threatened fatal consequences.

He had told his companion that there was no danger of disturbance from their enemies, and he really believed there was not, for the house was so far removed from the tract swept over by the Tories and Indians that the supposition was a reasonable one. The conclusion was a correct one on general principles; but there was the possibility that always hangs over every one—a chance turn in affairs, by which the peril would be precipitated.

The visit of the redskins was an accidental one, for they, too, committed the error of supposing there was no one in the dwelling—at least, belonging to the party whom they were hunting. Had there been a suspicion of anything different, those within would never have been apprised of the approach of their foes, except when too late.

The Mohawk had scarcely checked himself in his utterance, when he darted his hand forward, seized the wrist of the startled girl and drew her from the chair in which she was sitting. Without a second's pause, he hurried to the foot of the stairs, leaving the door open at the bottom, so that the Indians could ascend if they chose, without the least hindrance. In her trepidation, the girl reached out to draw the door shut after them, but the Indian would not allow her to touch it and hurried her upstairs, into the room from which he had signaled to her to come when she was waiting outside.

All that time—and it seemed long—the two could catch the sound of voices on the outside, so there could be no mistake about their enemies being close at hand, the peculiar intonation telling Lega-Wingo that they belonged to his own race. Once within the room above, the girl was led part way to the window, halting just where she could not look outside, and he whispered, "Stay there!"

She nodded her head to signify that she understood and would obey, and one long silent stride carried the lank body of the Mohawk to the window, out of which he peeped at the coming savages, concealing himself from sight with little trouble. The view only confirmed what his ear had told him. Some six or eight Iroquois were within the small yard surrounding the house, grunting and talking in a way that proved they had scarcely a thought of danger, or of finding any of the settlers in a place which showed at the first glance that it had been deserted long since by the owners.

It was a puzzle to Lena-Wingo why these warriors had paused here, and he made up his mind there was really no good cause, but that the call was merely a chance one. They were a band that had probably been attached to a larger one ravaging through the valley, or they were returning from some unusually long pursuit of the fugitives. As the day was very warm, it might be they had stopped to rest, in obedience to some whim. But all this was conjecture, and the great concern of the scout was as to how he was to get himself out of an exceedingly bad dilemma.

He saw that the Iroquois were about entering the house, and, having no fear of disturbance from the whites, they did not place a guard on the outside to watch for eavesdroppers, nor to prevent the flight of any who possibly might be waiting within. The Mohawk watched them as a cat watches a mouse, not allowing the slightest movement to escape him. It was this total lack of suspicion on the part of the visitors that opened the way for the display of the peculiar powers of Lena-Wingo.

Still keeping his own head concealed, he was able to tell, by using eyes and ears, the precise moment when the last enemy entered the room below. As soon as they crossed the threshold they would see the signs of the feast that had taken place so recently, and their suspicions would be aroused at once. At the very instant the last of the "Six Nations," as the Iroquois were called, had passed within the door the Mohawk seized Rosa Minturn by the arms. Before she could comprehend what he was trying

to do, he had forced her through the window—she
assisting the second she saw his purpose—and
holding her for a second or two by the hands that
her dress might settle in shape, and she might also
prepare for the fall, he let go. She dropped the
few remaining feet, striking so lightly that she
was not injured in the least.

Up to this time not a word had been exchanged
between the two nor was there now. As soon as
Rosa's feet struck the ground, she looked up to
her dusky friend for guidance. He pointed to the
clump of trees in which she had stood concealed a
short time before, as the direction for her to
follow. As proof that there was no time for
loitering, he not only pointed in that direction,
but he shot his finger a half dozen times with a
vigor that could not be misunderstood.

It seemed to the frightened girl that it was sure
death to make the attempt, but it was the same
to remain, and she did not hesitate. She headed
straight across the intervening space, and ran
with all the speed of which she was capable. It
seemed to her that after drawing in her breath, at
the moment of starting, she did not breathe
again until the trying run was ended. She did
not dare to look over her shoulder, for fear that

AND HOLDING HER FOR A SECOND OR TWO BY THE HANDS * * * HE
LET HER DROP — Page 164.

it might delay her steps. She was in that state of dread in which she expected every minute to hear the crack of a rifle aimed at her, or the sudden cry announcing she was discovered, and the fatal pursuit begun.

When it is remembered how peculiarly exposed she was to such discovery, it will seem almost incredible that she should escape; yet she did, and there was the soundest philosophy for her doing so, wherein lies the secret of that readiness of resource for which Lena-Wingo was distinguished. When Rosa sped across the open space, there were two windows in the room which the Iroquois had entered, and from which they could have seen the frightened fugitive had they but looked out at that critical time. No one understood this better than the Mohawk, and he prepared for the danger. He was certain, also that just as soon as the warriors stepped within the house, their attention would be arrested by the signs of the recent occupancy of it.

They would approach the little deal table, upon which were the remnants of the feast, and they were sure to spend several minutes in finding out what it all meant. These precious minutes were the ones which the Mohawk intended should be used by the girl in reaching shelter. The simple question with the dusky scout was whether the time allowed for this strange means of escape would be sufficient for the fleet-footed girl.

He watched her flight across the open space, and his dark eye kindled with admiration at her swift progress, for it struck him that she would need only a little more training to hold her own with some of the warriors themselves. The sagacity of the Mohawk was shown in the fact that the brief period upon which he counted for the safe flight of the girl proved sufficient for that purpose.

CHAPTER XXII.

EIGHT AGAINST ONE.

PROBABLY at no time since the Mohawk had undertaken to conduct Rosa to a place of safety was his anxiety on her account so great as when he stood by the open window of the deserted house, and watched her flight to the shelter of the group of trees a short distance away. While he viewed her motions, he also watched those of the redmen below. His keen sense of hearing, together with his intimate knowledge of their characteristics, enabled him to decide what they were doing almost as well as if he were looking down through the ceiling upon them.

He knew that the first one who entered the room caught the signs of the recent occupancy of the place, and apprised the others of the discovery at the same moment. Then, as they followed him stealthily in, they stood like so many bronze images, staring about the apartment, and using their eyes to find the explanation. When Rosa had reached a place of shelter, the time had come to dismiss her from his thoughts, and to attend to his own affairs.

One Indian against eight! Certainly the odds were alarming, even though the one at bay had the upper position, and was somewhat in the character of a defender. But Lena-Wingo possessed another advantage, on which he relied in a great degree. His enemies did not know who was in the building besides themselves, nor whether there was one or half a dozen. It was his purpose to keep up the deception, and, if possible, to increase it.

While those below-stairs were still standing motionless, and considering what was best to do, he moved his feet over the floor, softly it is true, but still distinctly enough to be heard by all, the sound being such as would be made by several persons trying to change their position without attracting the notice of their foes. This preliminary strategy was successful. The redmen were alarmed by the conviction that they had entered a house in which were a number of their foes. The question with them, as a consequence, became as to how they should extricate themselves from what looked like a dangerous situation.

They might make an advance upon the defenders

above-stairs, but to do that required a species of
courage which not one of them possessed, and the
Mohawk had little fear of their doing so. He
would not have cared had they made the attempt,
for he was confident that he could repel them as
they came within his reach. He therefore waited
composedly until the sounds from below should
tell him what they had decided to do. After a few
seconds of complete stillness, he detected faint,
muffled noises, which he knew were made by the
Indians moving steathily around the apartment.

A cellar was connected with the house, and there
were also other rooms reached from the one in
which they were standing. They were skirmishing about, to learn whether there were any whites
in other portions of the building than above-stairs.
It was necessary to manage the reconnoissance
with such care that some time was required before
it was completed. But the conclusion, as anticipated, was that the enemy was concentrated in
the upper story.

While they were thus employed, the Mohawk
was not idle. As there was no telling how long
he was likely to stay in his "castle," it was all-
important that he should learn its precise capaci-
ties in the way of defense. These did not prove to

be very extensive. The second story of the settler's building, which was taken possession of in this summary manner, consisted of two rooms and nothing more, there being no loft or attic to which one might retire, if compelled to retreat before the advance of the assailants from below. These apartments were of the simplest construction, all the furniture having been taken away, so there was nothing in the nature of a refuge to be used in case the enemy pressed him to the wall.

The Iroquois below seemed to reach the conclusion that it would not do for them to stay where they were, and the Mohawk had scarcely finished his reconnoissance when he found they were stealing out of the building altogether. This was not as he wished things to shape themselves, for it unquestionably placed him more on the defensive than before; but the scout met the new movement with the same coolness he had shown from the first. He foresaw that the struggle was likely to become a prolonged one, as some of his enemies would probably steal off in quest of reinforcements, especially if they discovered who he was.

If it should become known that they had brought the great Mohawk scout to bay, Colonel Butler would send half his men to secure him, even if he did not feel sure Rosa Minturn was in the same building with him. If found impossible to dislodge the warrior from his defense, there could be little doubt that the attempt would be made to burn him out; so, let events shape themselves as they might, Lena-Wingo considered it certain that lively times were at hand. It was his aim, as a matter of course, to keep his identity concealed as long as possible, and not to allow his enemies to know that he was the single defender of the house.

Ten minutes after he noticed the sounds that showed the Iroquois were withdrawing, he caught sight of one of them a hundred yards from the building. This was proof that the warrior had gone to that distance for the purpose of reconnoissance, and it suggested also that the situation of Rosa Minturn was becoming critical when their enemies were spreading out in the neighborhood. But for the time she must look out for herself, as the scout had his own hands full.

One of those tedious intervals that often characterized Indian warfare succeeded. For an entire hour a mere spectator would have decided that nothing at all was done. During this time the Mohawk held his position in the upper room, while the Iroquois maneuvered on the outside, their principal object being to learn something more definite of the number and intention of the garrison. It is hardly necessary to say that in this respect they were disappointed, and the deception was deepened.

Lena-Wingo, when he caught sight of three of the warriors standing on the edge of the wood, looking inquiringly toward him, and gesticulating in a way that showed they were engaged in an earnest discussion, sent a rifle ball among them, merely to apprise them the garrison was on guard. From the window on the opposite side of the apartment was sent another bullet, after a single Cayuga, who did not seem to suspect his danger, the two balls being fired so near together that not one of the warriors dreamed it possible they could have come from the same gun. In neither case was a warrior killed, for Lena-Wingo did not seek to bring them down, his object having been obtained by the simple act of firing.

At this critical juncture, however, an incident occurred that was as great a surprise to the defender of the house as to the assailants. The former had prepared for a desperate struggle

which would probably be continued into the
night, when the diversion came. Lena-Wingo
had just reloaded his piece, and was looking at
the group of three Indians who were still discussing him, when a gun was fired from a point in the
wood not far off, and one of the trio was seen to
throw up his arms and fall forward on his face.

CHAPTER XXIII.

AN UNEXPECTED ALLY.

WHOEVER fired the gun that brought down one of the three Iroquois had done it in the interest of the Mohawk, for certainly one of his deadliest enemies was laid low thereby. Sagacious and shrewd as was the dusky scout, he was unable to guess who his friend could be. He scrutinized the point from which the shot was fired so long and intently that he ran risk of being detected himself and drawing a shot.

The crack of the rifle was so unexpected by the Iroquois that it produced consternation among them. The two who escaped him leaped back into the woods, out of sight of the one who had fired the fatal shot. It was not long, however, before the Mohawk discovered them peering from behind the trees in the direction from which came the messenger of death.

While they were thus employed, two more warriors appeared between the spot where they were standing and the one from which the fatal bullet had been sent, apparently unaware of the critical position in which they placed themselves. But they were not long in learning their error, for they were no more than fairly in sight when from the same point on the edge of the forest was seen the little blue puff of smoke, and the report of the gun was scarcely sooner than the death cry of the Indian at whom it was aimed. This was effective work, and Lena-Wingo knew enough to reinforce it without delay.

Before the comrade of the one that had just fallen could get out of the way, he received a leaden messenger from the gun of the scout, who made his aim no less sure than the one that preceded it. And this was more effective work still; for it taught the Iroquois that they were "flanked," and caught between two fires. The result was a sort of panic, and those who were still unharmed hurried from the spot, without making any more investigation. Still, after such a repulse, they were likely to return with a larger force, and burn the building that had proved so disastrous to them.

Lena-Wingo could see no wisdom in staying to take part in the proceedings that were certain to follow, and he did not stay. Waiting a few minutes, to give the Iroquois enough time to get fairly under way, the scout vaulted out the window from which he had fired but a minute before, and, without hesitation, started on a rapid walk toward the point from which the two friendly shots had been fired. He had not reached it by several rods when the figure of a young man stepped forth, and smilingly greeted him.

"Well, Jack," said he, extending his hand, "it seems that I was just in time to do something for you, and I am glad of it. But how was it you were caught in such a fix?"

It was Ned Clinton, one of the young scouts, who thus addressed him, and the Mohawk grinned more than usual, as he shook the extended hand and replied:

"Stop there with girl to eat—Iroquois come—girl slip off—Lena-Wingo stay—Ned come—shoot good—they run—where he come?"

"Why, Jo and I have been skirmishing through the woods ever since the battle. We started for Wilkesbarre, and had got nearly there when Jo became so worried about his folks that he asked me to try to go back to Forty Fort, and find out whether it was all well with them; I was as anxious as he, and we started.

"Well, the woods are full of Indians and Tories, I can tell you, and we had a pretty tough time of it, but Jo succeeded in reaching his own house, where he heard the worst kind of tidings. He found his father and mother, who told him that you started with Rosa last night for Wilkesbarre, to get away from Colonel Butler, and he had sent a lot of Indians in pursuit, and they were afraid you would not be able to make it.

"It seems that one of the Tories had called at the house and given them the news, adding that Butler had sworn you should be scalped and Rosa brought back, and they were expecting the return of the pursuers every minute, with your scalp, but I guess they'll keep on expecting for some time yet."

The Mohawk grinned again at this compliment to his prowess, and said:

"Iroquois hunt for Lena-Wingo scalp many times—not got him yet—keep on hunt for him."

"Well, while Jo was in the house, I waited in the woods for him, for I was a little afraid of going in, as there were some of the Tories and Indians that don't love me any more than they ought, and I believed, if they saw both of us together, they would be more likely to interfere than if we were apart.

"Jo's folks wanted him to start with me after you, thinking we might be able to help you on the way to Wilkesbarre, when you had the girl to take care of.

"It took Jo a good while to get back to me in the woods, and, when he succeeded, we did not know what to do; but Colonel Denison had told him that you had said to him before starting that you meant to go pretty well up the river before crossing, and he believed that you had not gone over yet; so we picked our way up stream as best we could, and you need not be told that we had pretty hard work of it, running against some of the warriors twice, and narrowly missing being caught three times, but we managed to reach this place, where, as good fortune would have it, we met Rosa face to face, and she told us the whole story.

"She had waited and watched, in the hiding that you directed her to, until the redmen were beginning to spread out, so that she was in danger of being discovered, when she concluded the only thing she could do to save herself was to move further back into the woods, and it was while she was doing so that we met her and heard her story.

"As it looked as if you were in a bad place, it was agreed that Jo should go on up stream with his sister a little way, and after putting her in some good hiding-place, he was to come back and help me in trying to assist you. Before he could return, the necessity passed."

The eyes of the Mohawk sparkled in a manner that proved he was well pleased with the action of the young scouts.

"You and Jo do well—brave men."

"I don't know about that, but we were glad enough, I can assure you, to be able to do something for you, who have risked so much, and befriended us and our friends so often."

"If men all like you," added the red scout, "Colonel Butler and Iroquois and Tories all drive back —no white men scalp and tomahawk—we shoot 'em all."

A compliment from a hero like Lena-Wingo was the highest kind of tribute, and the young man blushed like a schoolboy at the consciousness that he had succeeded in winning the good opinion of the brave fellow. But business was on hand, and there was no time for delay.

"Jack, don't you think the Indians we have repulsed will be likely to return again, to drive us off, or, rather, to punish us for this little affair?"

"Yes—soon be here—soon come."

"Then we had better be on the move."

"Yes—we go—we no stay."

Nevertheless, the Mohawk did not seem to be in a hurry about moving off, though he had just admitted the necessity of doing so.

The reason was, that he was not only aware they would return, but he was quite certain of the time that would be required to bring them back; hence he knew the period that it was safe to remain.

"What would you have done if I had not been able to help you?" asked Ned, noticing his delay, but not desiring to claim any undue credit for the part he had played in extricating the Mohawk from his embarrassing predicament.

"Stay till night—then slip out—run away."

"But suppose they had fired the house? What then?"

"Lena-Wingo wouldn't let 'em," was the instant reply, with the old flash of the eye. "They come up to house to set fire—Lena-Wingo shoot 'em all."

"I have no doubt you would have managed to get along, for if half the stories told about you are true, you have been in a great many worse scrapes than that."

"Come," said the Indian abruptly. "We look for girl and Jo."

And the two moved off in the forest.

CHAPTER XXIV.

UNEXPECTED PERIL.

As is frequently the case in these days, the lightning struck where it was least expected. Neither Lena-Wingo nor Ned Clinton supposed that there was any danger to happen to Jo Minturn, who had taken temporary charge of his sister, and ordinarily, there would not have been. The meeting between the two was of the most affectionate character, for, despite the favorable news that reached the sister of the safety of her brother, she could not avoid a certain anxiety when there was such a terrible massacre going on all the time.

After the greeting between her and Ned, it will be understood that the latter went to the assistance of the Mohawk in the building, when the couple continued in quest of some hiding place for the girl, where she could be left, while Jo returned to the help of Ned in his efforts to save the friendly scout. It was a small matter to discover a place that would answer for the fair fugitive when there was such a growth of dense bushes and shrubbery. After going several hundred yards, they found themselves upon the banks of the Susquehanna, where Jo proposed that his sister should remain till he could return for her.

"Of course you will stay right here, Rosa," said he, "and not be tempted away by anything that may be going on near you?"

"Not unless I am driven off by some of the Indians or white men."

"I don't think you are in any danger from that, for the undergrowth is so thick that one might step on your dress without seeing you, and there is no possibility of any of the warriors trying to follow your trail."

"I have no fear for myself," replied the girl, as she entered the sheltering woods. "It is more on your account."

"Me?" laughed the young man. "What could have put such an idea in your head? Haven't Ned and I learned enough during the last few days to take care of ourselves? I tell you, Ned is a brave fellow, Rosa, and if it hadn't been for him, you would never have seen me again. But I mustn't stay here to talk, for he may want me to help him out."

Hastily embracing his sister, he kissed her good-bye, and, as he moved away, looked back and threw her a kiss at the moment the intervening shrubbery shut them from each other's sight.

Just as Jo started, the sound of the last shot of Lena-Wingo told him that something was up, and showed the proper direction to follow to reach his friends. The peculiar phase that the struggle between **the** Mohawk and his enemies took at that juncture was unsuspected by Jo, and was the cause of his getting into the worst kind of difficulty.

When the Iroquois became panic-stricken by the fire from front and rear and started in such haste for help with which to avenge themselves on their adversaries, several of them headed directly toward Jo, so that, unless something unexpected by either should intervene, they were sure to meet. Of course neither party was aware of his unfortunate state of the case, and nothing did intervene to avert the meeting.

Jo was walking quite rapidly in the direction of the point whence came the shooting, when he was startled by the sound of bodies moving through the woods in advance. He abruptly paused, not knowing what it meant.

"What's that, I won—"

There was no necessity of his wondering any further about the matter, for at that moment the figures of the four Iroquois appeared in the path, less than a hundred feet distant. They advanced so unexpectedly that the lad was entirely unprepared for them. Had he been given a single second's warning, he could have done something, for a large tree was within a yard of the very spot where he had halted. But the redmen caught sight of him at the same instant that he descried them, and, such being the case, concealment was out of the question.

Obviously, there was but one course open to the youth, and that was to whirl around and run as fast as he knew how. That he did, without stopping to consider which might be the wisest step, when there was but the one thing to do. The Indians, as may be supposed, were eager to secure some white man upon whom to wreak a partial revenge for what they had already suffered but a short time before. At the same instant, therefore, that Jo Minturn started to run they began an equally vigorous pursuit.

The danger to the young scout was imminent, for the Indians were fleet of foot, and were so

close at the instant he began his flight that there
was little chance for strategy or maneuvering.
With the sheltering shadows of the woods, and
the dense undergrowth, he would not have asked
a much greater start than he had secured, but the
few yards he lacked were the few that it seemed
could not be obtained. Feeling that all depended
upon his speed, Jo did his utmost. He went tear-
ing through the forest like one who knew his life
was the prize for which he was contending.

He could get over the ground with considerable
speed when he set about it, and for the first few
rods he not only held his own but slightly drew
away from his dusky pursuers.

Indeed he might have gained a chance to attempt
some of his tactics, but at the very moment he
was meditating doing so, he reflected that he was
speeding directly toward the hiding-place of his
sister, and was close to it already. If she learned
what was going on, she was likely to expose herself to an equally great danger, in the effort to
secure the assistance of the Mohawk or his friend.
And if that did not follow, there was the certainty
that he would betray her hiding-place to the very
miscreants who were hunting her.

This dread caused him to make a sudden turn to the left and up the river, but with no clearly defined purpose as to where he was to stop. His first thought was to make for the river, and to plunge into that, trusting to the extraordinary powers of swimming that had served him so well the night before. But his skill in that respect could have availed him nothing but for the favoring darkness, and it was evident to him that the result would be fatal, so far as he was concerned.

Then he fancied that by shouting at the top of his bent, he would bring Lena-Wingo to his assistance, provided the Mohawk was in a situation to respond. But Jo did not suspect these Iroquois belonged to the body that were pressing the red scout so hard, for the redmen were wandering everywhere in the forest and through the valley. This plan, likely, would have accomplished its purpose if tried, but it was abhorrent to the fugitive, who felt that it savored of cowardice, and it might give his pursuers more confidence than they now felt, and perhaps bring more of their comrades to the spot.

Not a shot had been fired as yet by the pursuing Iroquois, nor had they given utterance to a single outcry; but, feeling that the game was in their

hands, they settled down to the work of securing
it. Now and then—when the frightened fugitive glanced over his shoulder, he saw the warriors pressing him hard, none relaxing their
vigilance in the least. He was encouraged
by the belief at first that he was gaining ground,
but his heart sank when, a few minutes after
making his turn up the stream, he became convinced that the utmost he could do was to hold
his own. It seemed to Jo that something might
be accomplished by swerving in the direction of
the spot where he believed Ned Clinton and the
Mohawk were awaiting him. In fact, there was
nothing else left for him to try, and he tried it as
soon as it came to mind. But this scheme was to
be of no avail whatever in the peril in which he
was placed.

CHAPTER XXV.

THE SPIDER'S WEB.

By this time, the "second wind," as it is called, had come to Jo, and inspired by the belief that there was hope, he indulged in a burst of speed which almost instantly placed him so far beyond the Iroquois that the pursuers and pursued were lost to the sight of each other. This was encouraging in the highest degree, though it did not establish the safety of the fugitive by any means. He had succeeded in reaching that point where he only needed to get a little further to make his position almost secure, and where, at the same time, he only wanted to halt for a single minute to drop into the clutches of his enemies. Poor Jo strove as never before, and he was quite hopeful that he was drawing away from his foes, when he made another turn to the right, and exactly at the instant of doing so caught sight of a hollow tree before him.

He recognized it as one in which he had spent a night some time before, when hunting in this section. The interior was large enough to contain several men, the opening being on the other side. Without time enough to think of the rashness of trusting to such a shelter when the Iroquois were at his heels, the lad dashed around the trunk and crawled within as nimbly as if he was a coon with a pack of hounds after him. The moment that the fugitive was inside, his heart sank, for he felt he had committed a fatal mistake; but it was two late to withdraw, and he could only wait until they came up and took him prisoner.

The hole by which he had entered this hollow was some four or five feet from the ground, but of such dimensions that he was able to go in without difficulty. The tree itself was a large one, the trunk being several feet in diameter, so that as he shrank into the furthest part possible, the thought came to him that there was room for two or three more beside him. The interior was as dark as night, the faint sunlight penetrating only a few inches within the opening by which the fugitive had made his way into the strange retreat.

The instant he was backed against the other side of the trunk, he crouched down so as to place his head below the possible range of light, and waited for the Iroquois to come and take him; for he had made up his mind that there was no use of resistance, while, by surrendering, he might gain time for the Mohawk to help him out The lad had scarcely taken his positin, when he noticed a spider busily engaged in spreading its net across the door through which he had come.

"I suppose I ruined some of his work when I entered in such a hurry," was the thought of the boy, "and he is in haste to repair his house."

All this, it will be understood, occupied but a very few seconds. As the Iroquois had not abated their pursuit in the least, Jo was scarcely given time to notice the singular work of the spider, when he heard the patter of the moccasins on the leaves, showing that they were close at hand and making straight for his hiding-place.

The lad felt the faintest possible hope that the redmen might run by without noticing the opening in the tree, as it was not noticeable until they were nearly opposite or beyond. But this hope was dissipated the next moment, when the sounds of the feet showed they had stopped running and were walking—a thing they would not do if they believed the young scout still on the wing.

They had observed the large tree with its inviting opening and were too wise to pass it without examination; but, to the great surprise of Jo, he heard them speaking not in their own tongue, but in broken English.

"He go in dere," said one, no doubt referring to the hole.

"Yes, we got him," assented another. "He run hard, he crawl in dere to rest—we make him rest."

The warriors no doubt spoke in this tongue that the cowering fugitive might understand them, and suffer all the agony of one who feels that his doom cannot be averted. They indulged in several more observations, relating mainly to what they intended to do when they should haul the poor "Yankee Dog" from his hiding-place. The boy suffered death over and over again, and wished they would draw him forth and end his terrible suspense. He even meditated rising, crawling out and surrendering to them.

The dreadful trial lasted but a few minutes when one of the Iroquois advanced and looked in. Standing in the light as he did, his painted face was brought out in relief, and Jo was sure that in his experience of the past few days he had not seen anything to compare with it in hideous atrocity of expression. Before this warrior said anything more, he thrust his head into the opening, with a view of examining the interior and satisfying himself of the precise position of their victim. As he leaned forward with this purpose, the gauzy web that had been spun across the fissure crossed his nose, and he drew back, straightened up, and pinched the meshes between his fingers, calling the attention of the others to the fact, using the language this time of his own people.

His companions gathered about him, and for a few minutes there was an earnest consultation. The youngest boy knows, that, as a rule, the spider's web, when torn away, is not instantly replaced—certainly not when the author of the ruin is at hand and ready to repeat the destruction; and so, when we see an abundance of spider webs, we take it as evidence that the place has not been disturbed very recently. And this was the exact conclusion reached by the Iroquois when they observed that the hole in the trunk was crossed by the meshes of a spider's web. Nothing was plainer to them than that this retreat had not been visited by any one for some time past. The fugitive whom they were hunting must have

gone by, and was still running for life, while they
were frittering away their time under the belief
that they were adding to his misery. The web
convinced them that they had made a blunder,
and, without pausing for further examination of
the hiding-place, they resumed the pursuit with
greater vigor than before.

Jo Minturn, therefore, was saved by a spider
web. The young fugitive could scarcely believe
what had taken place until the Iroquois were gone
and he was left alone. The cause of their mistake
was too apparent to be overlooked.

Waiting a few minutes, he peeped out of the
opening, and, seeing a clear coast, lost no time in
crawling forth from such quarters and leaving the
vicinity.

"That was a wonderful escape," he thought, as
he walked along. "It does seem that Providence
interferes in a way that no one could dream of.
Ten minutes ago I did n't believe there was any
possible means for me to get out, except by a mira-
cle, and it came."

God helps those who help themselves, and Jo
tried hard to remember that danger was on every
hand, and it was never safe to forget it for a
moment. The most natural course for him to fol-

low was to make his way back to where he had left his sister, and this he proceeded to do at once. He remembered the place so well that there could be no mistake, and he was in high spirits, anxious to tell his good fortune before he started in quest of Lena-Wingo and Ned Clinton. He reached the spot in a short time, but his consternation knew no bounds when he made the discovery that she was not there!

CHAPTER XXVI.

ALL ABROAD.

Young Minturn was taken all aback when he reached the margin of the Susquehanna, at the precise spot where he had left his sister, only to discover that she was gone.

"She promised she would not stir from here, unless she was forced to do so," he said to himself, after repeating the hunt several times, "and it must have been some danger that drove her away."

Hoping that she might be somewhere in the vicinity, he ventured to pronounce her name several times in a voice loud enough to be heard a few rods off, but he was apprehensive of the result of such a course, and did not keep it up very long. Nothing of the nature of a response was heard, and the conviction was inevitable that she had gone—who could say where? The most natural supposition was that some of the Iroquois, who seemed to be everywhere, had been guided by evil fortune to her hiding-place, and had taken her captive. The thought was disheartening, but the anguish smitten brother was helpless and without any power, so far as he could see, to help her. He could not make sure even of the direction taken by her and her captors. There remained the faint hope that she had discovered the approach of peril in time to take refuge elsewhere, and that as soon as her enemies were gone, would return to her old concealment. It was this hope that prevented the brother from leaving the spot, and threw him into an agony of doubt as to what he ought to do.

The passage of each minute caused this possibility to become less and less, until at the end of half an hour scarcely any remained. The poor fellow was in a most distressing quandary. A little while before it seemed that he was the only one who was in a situation from which there was no escape, and now it appeared to him that he was the sole member of the little party who was actually safe from the Tories and Indians. He had not been able, as yet, to go to the help of Ned Clinton and Lena-Wingo, and therefore could know nothing about the manner in which they had gotten out of the beleaguered building. Much as they might need his aid, he felt that his sister possessed the first claim, as they themselves would insist, if they knew all.

He made as careful examination of the ground as he knew how, in the hope of gaining some inkling of what had taken place, but his experience in the forest was not sufficient to read these signs as Lena-Wingo would have done, had he been present. The leaves were rumpled as if by the passage of several feet, but it was impossible to distinguish whether it was done by those of a lady, himself, or an enemy.

"I don't see that I can do anything," he reflected, after his suspense had continued for half an hour; "I shall have to wait till Ned and the Mohawk come here, or hunt them myself, and get them to help me out."

It was past noon, and he looked upon the approach of night with a dread impossible to describe.

"If she isn't found before dark," he added, sitting down upon the trunk of a fallen tree, in gloomy reverie, "I shall make up my mind that it is all over with the poor girl. The idea of her being in the hands of the Iroquois is enough to drive me wild. Colonel Butler has sent them to hunt for her, and as like as not, they won't take her back to him. They are so enraged against all the settlers in the valley that they will tomahawk her as they have done many a time when given prisoners to bring in."

The brother, it will be seen, was lifted from the highest ground of hope, only to be thrown into the lowest depths of gloom and despair. The thought that he was powerless to do anything to help his beloved sister was almost unbearable. If there was any way, no matter how desperate, for him to strike a blow for her, he would seize it at once; but, as it was, he could only wait and pray for some such opening to come to him. When this suspense had lasted a half hour longer, it became intolerable, and he sprang to his feet.

"What's the use?" he exclaimed. "I may stay here all day and night, and that will be all there is of it. If Red Jack won't come to me, I'll go to him."

And with this determination, he strode off in the direction from which came the shots heard some time before. He walked hurriedly, for, since he had made up his mind to take this course, he was impatient with himself that he had delayed so long in setting about it. There could be no mistake about the route he ought to pursue, and he did not forget the lesson learned from the spider's web. Despite his haste, he kept a sharp watch for enemies, and now and then came to a halt, that he might look and listen the better.

"I don't hear or see anything of them," he added, when he had paused in this manner some six or eight times; "but that's no proof that a score of them are not within a hundred yards of this very spot, waiting till I walk into some of their traps. I wish the Mohawk would show up, for if his help was ever needed, now is the time."

Picking his way in this careful fashion, it was not long before he became aware that he was approaching an open space, probably the very house and clearing he was seeking. A few rods further, and he stopped, for he had penetrated as far as seemed prudent, and was looking upon the very dwelling from which Rosa had escaped by such a narrow chance, and where the Mohawk, Lena-Wingo, had stood at bay before eight Iroquois, until the diversion created by the coming of Ned Clinton gave him the chance to flee. Jo identified it from the description received from his sister, as well as from his own knowledge of its location.

"I don't see anything of them," he said to himself, after watching the building a short time. "I wonder whether the scout has given them the slip, or whether they have him locked in there?"

While he was wondering what the stillness that hung over everything could mean, he made the alarming discovery that there were at least a score of Iroquois in the immediate vicinity, with undoubted designs upon the house. These were the reinforcements for which the small party that received the repulse had gone, and they were now on hand. As good fortune would have it, most of them were on the side of the wood nearly opposite to where the lad was standing, well screened by the trees. So long, therefore, as he exercised ordinary prudence, he could keep out of their way and watch their proceedings.

It will be remembered that Jo had not been given any chance to learn of the clever style in which the smaller party was repulsed by Lena-Wingo and Ned Clinton, and he was held to the spot by his anxiety as to the fate of both. If the two were in the house, then it was very plain to him that they were to go through the hardest kind of struggle to escape their enemies, and it looked as if he was likely to play a part in the programme.

"If Jack is there," he muttered, as he scrutinized the upper windows, "he must know that the Iroquois are here, and I am surprised that he does n't give them a shot, just to wake them up."

A few minutes after the redmen who were stealing along the other side of the clearing, sent in three or four shots, designed to bring out a reply from the garrison—a desire which our readers will understand could not be gratified, for the best of reasons. In a little while two guns were discharged from another point, but as before, the marksmen looked in vain for the response thereto.

CHAPTER XXVII.

BEHIND THE TREES.

Jo watched the proceedings before him with the closest interest, for they concerned his friends, and indirectly his missing sister. To the young scout, the silence of the Mohawk and Ned Clinton was inexplicable, except on the theory that they had escaped from the house by some means unknown to the redmen themselves. Had he but understood how the assailants had acted, he could have had no doubt on that point. As it was, the belief became almost a certainty, when another volley was fired by the Iroquois without producing any response from the house of the settler.

No doubt, the same suspicion was taking shape in the minds of the warriors, for they gradually became more bold, and finally took little care to shelter themselves behind the trees to which they had clung so tenaciously at the opening of the fight. A half dozen emerged from the wood, and walked directly out upon the clearing, as if inviting the garrison to fire upon them if they dared.

Had Lena-Wingo been there, he would have allowed such a challenge to pass unnoticed. The fact that the stillness was continued unbroken from the house made them bolder than ever.

More issued from the forest until the whole twenty were in view, and then several, rifle in hand, walked toward the building, never pausing till they were within the yard, at which time they indulged in further scrutiny of the structure before entering. Jo saw the leader suddenly make a dash within, and the others followed, as if they were a flock of sheep. They were not very quiet, either, for in the stillness of the summer afternoon the watcher could hear them tramping through the interior. In a short time they made a thorough survey of all the rooms, when a number appeared at the upper window. From the latter came a dismal howl,—one of disappointment,—for they had made the discovery that the birds had flown, having executed the not very brilliant maneuver of getting out when the chance was given them.

The young scout knew as well as they what the outcry meant, and it showed him there was no further occasion for his staying there. He paused a moment, however, to see how the Iroquois would take their disappointment, and he was not com-

pelled to wait long. In a short time they set fire
to the house, which, being made entirely of wood,
while the weather was very dry, burned with
great rapidity, and another landmark was left to
show where the Indians of Colonel Butler had
united with the Tories in the desolation of the fair
valley of Wyoming.

Jo did not wait longer, as time was precious,
and the most important thing he could do was to
hunt up the Mohawk, and appeal to him in turn
to hunt up Rosa. There were no means of deter-
mining which way the red scout had gone. But,
believing it likely that he would manage to make
his way to the place where the girl had been left in
hiding, the distressed brother started in that
direction.

"I don't see that there is any use of my trying
to do anything," he muttered, forgetting, in his
own misery, the wonderful manner in which he had
been extricated from a greater danger than that
which probably hung over his sister. "Ned and
the Mohawk have got away, that's pretty sure,
but how it is to help Rosa is more than I can
understand. They are likely to go tramping
about the woods till night comes again, and by
that time Butler will have her, if he hasn't now.

I don't know as the Mohawk could have managed better," he added, more reflectively, feeling a little compunction lest he should wrong the faithful Lena-Wingo, even in thought. "Colonel Denison tells me that Butler has taken a fancy to Rosa, and is determined to get his hands on her, so as to take her from us. He is wicked enough to do anything, and where he has so many Tories and Indians to help him, I don't see that we have much chance to beat him. If we manage to get over the Susquehanna, I don't know as we'll be safe at Wilkesbarre, for they may follow us there, and there is no reason to prevent their taking the place just as they swooped down on Wyoming—"

How much longer this gloomy soliloquy would have continued it is hard to say, had it not been broken in upon by an outsider. The young man had paused and was leaning against a tree, when a rustling among the leaves a short distance ahead warned him that he was not alone. Without waiting to finish his remark, he sprang behind the trunk, so as to interpose it between him and the stranger. That the latter was a redskin, fully as cautious as the young scout himself, was shown by his action; for he, too, leaped to cover, vanishing as suddenly as if the earth had opened and swallowed him up. This was proof, too, that the Indian was as quick to detect danger as was the white, and, sheltered now behind the tree, he was also as ready as him for the encounter.

Jo was apprehensive of the result of a struggle like this, for he knew how stealthily and cautiously one of these savage enemies would fight for the mastery. It was not at all unlikely that the Indian would keep out of sight till dark. Unless he could take the lad off his guard before that time, he would watch every movement of the adversary for hours never relaxing his vigilance, and ready to fire as soon as the slightest chance was given. Jo did not fancy the prospect of staying there till night, and he determined to leave, if possible.

His first essay to draw the fire of his enemy was the old one which all our readers have heard long ago. He placed his cap on the end of his ramrod and shoved it just far enough from behind the tree to make it appear that the owner was trying to take a peep at his enemy, thereby exposing his head to his marksmanship. But it wouldn't work. In common language, the artifice was "too thin" to deceive the wary redskin pitted against him. No answering shot told the youth that the barrel of his enemy's gun was empty, and he had only to rush out and shoot him before he could reload. The Indian continued silent and invisible, and the conviction stole over Jo that he must take a new tack.

The temptation to indulge in a stolen glance at the warrior was too great to be resisted; and, determined not to allow his curiosity to get the better of his caution, the lad moved his head very slowly forward, so as to permit the faintest possible look at the place where his foe had taken refuge. The tree was a large one—larger, indeed, than his own, and the distance between the two was over a hundred yards, so that if the youth should gain a chance to shoot his adversary, it was all-important to make his aim accurate, it being evident that a miss in a case like this would be equivalent to receiving the bullet of his foe. After a few minutes' careful maneuvering, Jo got his head so far around the tree that one eye was fixed on the trunk behind which the savage was standing.

Nothing was to be seen of him, though there could be no doubt the warrior was there. The invisibility of the redskin did not tempt the young

man into exposing any more of himself to his aim
than he could avoid. What threatened to become
a contest of mere watchfulness, and thereby
monotonous in spite of its dangerous nature,
proved to be much shorter than Jo anticipated.
He had not gazed long in the direction of his foe,
when he was certain he detected a movement
behind the tree itself—that is, beyond where it
would be supposed the warrior was standing.

Precisely what it was he could not determine,
but was certain that something was going on in
which he was interested, and which he ought to
understand. The impression made upon the lad
was as if the shadow of some bird or animal
had flashed before his eyes. He had not a particle
of doubt that it bore some relation to a maneuver
of the Indian, and that his life, perhaps, depended
upon his learning what it was and preparing
against it. All that he could do was to keep up
an unremitting watch, in the hope of discovering
something more, which would explain what it
meant. This watch continued less than fifteen
minutes, when it ended in the complete success of
the stratagem of the redman. .

CHAPTER XXVIII.

THE DEPTH OF SORROW.

YOUNG Minturn did not see the movement which puzzled him so much repeated, and of which he caught such an unsatisfactory glimpse. The reason why it was not done again was because once was sufficient. The Indian's purpose was to steal from behind the tree, and reach another position that would command that of the youth. He had therefore made a backward movement, almost flat on the ground, and, by a series of skillfully managed maneuvers, took a circuitous and stealthy march to the right, describing an arc of thirty degrees at least, and executing it with so much care that he was not only undetected, but was not even suspected of any such intent. When the warrior rose to his feet again, he stood almost behind the young scout, and in a position to enable him to send the bullet of his rifle crashing through his skull. The first warning that Jo received of his danger, was the crack of a gun from the rear, and the bullet chipped off the bark within an inch of his face.

THE INDIAN WAS IN FULL VIEW.—Page 211.

" You've missed," called out the lad, "and now take the consequences!"

But the next minute he changed his mind, and concluded he would not fire at all. The Indian was in full view, and it looked the easiest thing in the world to bring him down, but the trouble was that the redman standing before him was Lena-Wingo, the Mohawk. The scout had indulged in this sport for the purpose of testing the skill of his young friend, and with the object of teaching him a thing or two.

In leaving the tree in the first place, he had done it with the intention of giving Jo an inkling of what he was about, but the lesson was rather too "advanced" for the pupil to comprehend at the time. The painted face was one broad grin, as the Mohawk witnessed the amazement of the lad, who stared in speechless astonishment.

"Why, Jack, is that you?" he exclaimed, when his wits came back to him. "I've been hunting for you, and would have given the world, if I could, to have met you awhile ago."

"I'm here—what young man want?"

"Where is Rosa?"

Jo expected a favorable answer, so great was his trust in the wonderful skill of the Mohawk;

but the expression of his thin face, through its paint, told him the dreadful tidings before he answered.

"Lena-Wingo does not know—thinked she be with you."

"O, Heavens!" wailed the brother, almost falling to the earth in his great grief; "then the Iroquois have her!"

"What's that you say?"

It was Ned Clinton who asked the question, as he sprang from behind another tree, where he had been watching the little game of his friend the Mohawk.

"Rosa is gone!" was the faint response.

Ned clutched his arm, and hoarsely demanded:

"How is this? Tell us about it!"

"Yes—tell all—be quick," added Lena-Wingo, mastering his emotion in a way that he had learned in years of the most bitter kind of experience. "Be quick—tell all."

As soon as Jo could command his feelings sufficiently to speak with anything like coherence, he related what the reader has learned long since. While he spoke, the others listened with an intensity of interest that cannot be described, for the tidings was new to both.

After Ned and Red Jack got clear of the house, it will be recalled that they set out in quest of their friend Jo. Various difficulties conspired to prevent their getting on his track, and feeling no doubt that the girl was somewhere in the safe keeping of her brother, it was their intention to delay the crossing of the Susquehanna until dark. This theory will explain why it was that when they did catch sight of Jo, they felt warranted in taking time for the little test we have described.

It might well be a question which of the three individuals suffered the most from the uncertainty of the fate of Rosa Minturn. The brother was smitten to the earth by sorrow over what seemed to be the loss of one of the dearest and best sisters that was ever given to a lad. Ned Clinton was of that age when, under the dawnings of a young love, a pure and holy halo wrapped the maiden in all his dreams by night as well as by day. What though the gentle passion that pervaded and warmed with its vivifying glow his whole nature had never found expression from his lips, even to his dearest friend—what though the sweet imaginings that came to him in the stillness of the night, in the glare of the noonday, when in the wild tumult of battle, when he was swimming in the darkness the broad Susquehanna, or when threading his way through the trackless forest— what though these visions of his love, in all their entrancing beauty, were considered too sacred to be whispered to any mortal? They were none the less real and soul-stirring for all that. The grief that smote the brave youth was like the sweep of the cyclone, which brings low the tallest oak of the wilderness.

It seemed that he must die if the girl was taken from him, either by death or the still ruder hand of the sacrilegious Tory chief. How eagerly he had entered into the struggle of the colonies for their freedom, impelled not alone by his patriotism, which of itself was of the most exalted character, but spurred on also by the hope that when the independence of his dear country was gained—as gained it would surely be—it would be his blissful pleasure to come back to Wyoming valley, and, beating his sword into the plowshare, hear from Rosa the thrilling words:

"Well done, good and faithful servant! You have earned the love I now give you."

This was the ambition of the sturdy youth, and, to see its realization, he was ready to brave danger, hardship, and death itself. And now,

when on the threshold of the career he had
marked out for himself, to have the whole fabric
swept away by the remorseless hand of fate was
a blow which he could not bear! But he could
tell his sorrow to no one, for he knew that no one
could appreciate it.

Little did he dream that his friend, Jo Minturn,
suspected his secret, and perhaps it was as well
that he knew it not. He must keep his overwhelming sorrow to and within himself. More
than that, he must so act that no one could learn
its existence. It was an almost superhuman task,
but the stuff in the young patriot was that of
which heroes are made, and he resolved that it
should be done.

And much less could Lena-Wingo, the Mohawk
scout and tried friend of the whites, impart his
anguish to any confidant. There are curious
ambitions in this world, leading men by different
paths to face all manner of peril and death.
Years had now passed since he had foresworn his
own race, and devoted his life to proving himself
an ally of the whites, and he had pursued that
single course until it was the sole aim and object
of his existence—the goal to reach which he bent
all the energies of a nature peculiarly fitted for

such a work. In ways innumerable had he proven his affection, until affection itself was forgotten in the great passion. When he undertook a task for the white settlers, he would suffer nothing to divert him therefrom. Hunger, thirst, hardship, danger, sickness, disaster, gloom, storm, and sunshine, were all the same to him when once started on the path he laid out for himself.

To the Mohawk, failure was more ignominious than death. Having started for Wilkesbarre with the declaration that he would take Rosa there, he was confronted by the prospect of an utter overthrow of his plans. No earthly disgrace could be greater. If defeated in his purpose, he felt he would not be fit to show his face among men again, and it may be doubted whether he would ever be seen more if it should be that he was to prove unable to keep the pledge he had made to the parents of the missing maiden.

CHAPTER XXIX.

GROPING IN THE FOREST.

WE have omitted to tell one motive that, in the case of the Mohawk scout, would have led him to brave anything for the sake of saving Rosa Minturn, and that was the affection he entertained for her. No nature, however rugged and seemingly heartless, is without a tender spot which is susceptible to the gentler influences that distinguish man from the brute. While Lena-Wingo was ready at all times to do what in him lay for the good of the whites, there were necessarily a few upon whom he looked with a peculiar and unusual friendship.

Rosa Minturn was one of these—precisely why, it would be hard to tell, more than it would be to explain the birth and growth of love itself in the heart of Ned Clinton. It may have been because the warrior had always been a favored guest in the family, that he had seen her grow up from infancy; had played with her from the time she began to walk, had taken her with him on many

an excursion in the great wilderness that at that
day surrounded the lovely valley of Wyoming;
but more probable that in the nature of the beautiful child there was something akin to his own.
There was a certain innate bravery of disposition,
a self-possession in trying circumstances, a nim-
bleness of foot and limb, a power to withstand
fatigue, a love for the free, untrammeled life of the
woods, and daring, resolute character, which
never transgressed true feminine and modest
bounds, that made her a maiden above all others
in his estimation.

At the risk of being misunderstood, it may be
said that when the Mohawk left the house of Lorimer Minturn, near Forty Fort, he was in no hurry
to reach Wilkesbarre. In the first place, he believed
there was no doubt that the refuge would be made
without trouble. In short, he never considered
anything more certain than that they would
arrive there in spite of all that Colonel Butler and
his allies could do to prevent it. The journey
itself he looked upon in the nature of an excursion, and, well aware of the grit of the girl, he
meant that she should have a taste of frontier life
such as she had never known before. Although a
fair construction of the mishap might acquit the

Mohawk of all culpability, still he looked upon himself as the sole author of the calamity.

Within a tenth of the time taken to tell the story, Lena-Wingo had decided on his course of action. The red hero had been trained in the ways of his people too long to allow any one to read in his face the workings of his mind.

When Jo Minturn had finished his short account of what had befallen him, Lena-Wingo was as calm as when he stood in the house of the missing one the night before, discussing their plans with her parents and with Colonel Denison. He marked the woe that crushed the hearts of his two companions, but he offered no words of sympathy, for the reason that he held little faith in sentiment. It was the time for action, not words.

"We go where she was—where you left her—can you lead the way?"

"I came from there but a short time ago," replied Jo; "I can take you to the exact spot."

"Take us."

"Yes, lead the way," added Ned Clinton; "it is upon Jack, under Heaven, that we must now rely."

The lad wheeled on his heel as the words were spoken, and started off like one who knew the value of time. Fast as he strode, the Mohawk instantly dropped into a gait that compelled him to increase it.

"Was it by river?" he asked, noticing the course taken.

"It was."

"That bad," was the significant comment. "Iroquois come there—maybe find her."

The distance was not great to the stream, and it was soon reached, though at a point below the hiding-place of her for whom they were seeking.

"Look out—Injuns may be here!" admonished the Mohawk, slackening his speed when the river was placed on their right.

A few minutes after they halted at the very spot where the brother and sister had parted some two or three hours before.

"Here is where I left her," said Jo, "and when I came back to join her she was nowhere to be seen, and all traces of her were lost.

Lena-Wingo made no answer to this, for the point was now reached where he was to see what he could do for the lost one. He looked keenly around, and then, by several questions, learned the manner in which the girl was expected to spend the time during the absence of her brother. This was all, and he began a minute examination of the ground where it was certain she had trod.

To one of his vision and experience, it was no difficult matter to separate the footprints made by the delicate tread of Rosa from those of the other sex. His companions were watching his movements with the closest attention, and they saw him glide back and forth, with his head bent over, thinking of and seeing nothing but the almost invisible signs upon the leaves before him. His friends did not ask him a question, though many of his actions were not understood, for they knew that they would receive no notice while he was thus occupied. Accordingly, Jo and Ned sat down on the fallen tree, gloomy and dispirited, while they observed his course.

"Do you think there is any hope of his doing anything?" asked Jo, when the singular actions of the redskin had continued some time.

"I trust so," was the answer, uttered in a voice which showed the foundation therefor was very slight. "You know that if there is any way of finding her again, Jack is the one to do it."

"Yes, but if the thing can't be done, that's all there is about it."

"We're figuring all the while on the supposition that she has fallen into the hands of Butler, or some of the Indians, and yet we may be mistaken. Perhaps she concluded the spot was becoming too dangerous for her, and withdrew while there was time, and is at no great distance from here."

"If that were so, it seems she ought to have been back long ago, for there are no Indians here, nor have there been for a long time past. She knew that I would return to this spot to look for her, and she knew, too, how unlikely it was that I could follow her anywhere else."

There was reason in this theory, and Ned felt it was more probable than any other. Still, the fact that the Mohawk had gone to work with so much vigor and spirit was not without its effect upon his companions, who had pinned great faith to him for a long time.

"I feel very sorry for your *parents*," said Ned, a sort of instinct teaching him to parry the possible supposition that he was more stricken over the absence of the maiden than he ought to be. "Like everybody else, they have had no doubt that if Jack started for the place across the river he was sure to reach there, and the disappointment will be all the greater."

"I have thought once or twice that it might be Rosa has gone off so far that, when she tried to return, she went astray, and that while she is doing all she can to get back to the place where she knew I was waiting for her, yet she could not do so."

"It's possible, you know, Jo, that it is all well with her, in spite of the probabilities against it. While there's life there's hope, and, though I couldn't see the least light a while ago, I now begin to feel more hope than before."

"I wish I could," was the doleful reply of the brother, who was in as despairing a state of mind as can be conceived.

"We have several hours yet before night, and during that time there's no telling what may happen. Hello! Jack has made a discovery."

CHAPTER XXX.

A DISCOVERY.

THE cause of this exclamation on the part of Jo Minturn was a very simple movement of Red Jack, the Mohawk. During the few minutes that the scout was engaged in the search, he was bent in a stooping position, moving slowly from point to point, peering at the signs on the ground, too faint to be distinguished by other eyes. He now straightened up and uttered the single exclamation:

"Woofh!"

When he did so he was close to the river shore, and he turned his face around toward the young men, as if inviting them to join him—an invitation which they instantly accepted.

"See there," he added, pointing to the ground before them, where there was a place comparatively free from leaves. "Look at him."

It was several seconds before the youths understood to what he referred. But by bending almost to the earth, both saw the small, graceful outline of a lady's shoe, such as Cinderella might have made, had she passed that way.

"Rosa's footprints!" exclaimed her brother; "but what good is that to us? What are we to gain by it?"

"It shows that she went toward the river," answered Ned, taking his cue from the Mohawk, who was following the faint trail in that direction. "It gives the very information we want."

Lena-Wingo had worked hard at the clue, and was a little surprised to learn that it led in the direction of the stream, for he had another theory in his mind. Before he reached the water's edge he made a second discovery, which he did not communicate to his friends. Beside the footprints of Rosa Minturn there were those made by Indian moccasins. This boded ill for the girl, but he had partly expected it, and no exclamation told the others that he had come upon anything unusual.

The different tracks were so mingled together that it was impossible to tell whether those of Rosa were made at the same time or before those of the redmen. He was inclined to believe the girl, at that time, was a prisoner in the hands of the Iroquois, though it was by no means impossible that they were a half hour behind her. He

carefully tracked the footprints until they were
ended by the river itself, where, of course, they ter-
minated by entering a boat.   Had the warriors
and their captive stepped into the same canoe?

This was the great question, and Lena-Wingo
felt himself able to answer it, after a careful examination.   The problem was a simple one, and the
conditions were these: The footprints of the girl
disappeared, and a search for some distance up
and down stream failed to discover them again.
The trail of the Iroquois showed there were three
of them, stepping in the tracks of the maiden, and
the Mohawk had searched but a few minutes
when they came to view again.   This settled that
point.

When Rosa Minturn left the shore in a canoe,
she was alone—that was as certain as that the
sun was shining.   This news was good enough for
the Mohawk to turn about and explain to his companions.   The latter could not but be encouraged
by the certainty that Rosa had left the spot in a
boat, guided by her own hand, and not as a prisoner.   But to Ned and Jo the cause of her taking
such a course was as great a mystery as ever.

"It may be that she has crossed the river," suggested young Clinton, as his eye ranged along the opposite shore.

The possibility had suggested itself to Lena-Wingo, and caused him to search the wooded bank in quest of some signal from the girl, who, if there, ought to be looking out for the appearance of her friends on the other side. But the south-eastern shore was apparently as deserted as if never trodden by the foot of man. This failure to see anything of the fair fugitive led Lena-Wingo to believe she had not crossed the Susquehanna, without taking into account the extreme improbability of her attempting such a course in broad daylight, and when she must know that it was in direct opposition to the wishes of her friends.

The three stood for several minutes in consultation, or, more properly, the youths respectfully waited while their older companion deliberated on the next step he ought to take. The lovely summer afternoon was wearing away, and in a few more hours night would again descend upon the valley. Within the short period that still remained of daylight, they felt that whatever was done for Rosa Minturn must be done quickly. If darkness should wrap the earth in its mantle, and she still remain lost to them, the chances would be almost entirely against her recovery.

It being quite well settled that Rosa had not crossed the Susquehanna, it followed that the course to pursue was either up or down the bank on which they were standing.

There was no data to guide them, and the Mohawk could only proceed on general principles. It seemed to him the girl would conclude that there was less danger in going up than down the stream, as the former course would lead her further from Forty Fort, the starting point of her pursuers, while the latter would take her back over the same ground they had traversed during the forenoon. This course of reasoning decided the red scout to make his first search up the river shore; but to economize time he determined to send the two young men to hunt in the opposite direction.

"Walk slow," said he, in making known his wishes; "make no noise, watch for Iroquois, and watch for canoe."

"Suppose we catch sight of it, Jack, what then?" asked Ned Clinton.

"Come look for Lena-Wingo—he tell what do."

With this understanding the parties separated. The Mohawk, as may be supposed, was more expeditious in what he did than were his friends. As he went up the river shore, he proceeded very nearly as rapidly as when making his way through the wilderness at his ordinary gait. He could do this and guard against running into danger as well as if his walk was only half as fast.

He believed that if Rosa had taken this course, she would not have proceeded more than a couple of hundred yards before coming into land again. But, to leave no room for mistake on his part, he never paused until he had traveled fully twice that distance, at the end of which he came to the conclusion that, as he had discovered nothing at all, she must have taken the other course.

While he was thus employed, Jo Minturn and Ned Clinton were doing what they could to unravel the mystery of Rosa's whereabouts. Proceeding at a more tardy rate, they had not gone half as far as Lena-Wingo, when he turned to retrace his steps. But the result was the discovery that they had taken the right route. It was something like half the distance we have

spoken of, that they learned an important fact.
Ned was slightly in advance of his companion,
walking with the utmost caution, neither of the
two having spoken a word, when he paused.

"What's up?" asked Jo, in a whisper.

Ned answered him by stealthily parting the
bushes immediately in front with one hand, while
he pointed down stream with the other, still
silent, as if fearful that a whisper might betray
them. There it was, no more than fifty feet away.
Drawn up against the shore was a small canoe,
its nose resting against the bank, just far enough
to keep it from being carried away by the current.
The young scouts stood several minutes contem-
plating it, without stirring or speaking. Then
Ned said:

"That's the boat we are looking for, and what
shall we do?"

"Let's examine it."

"I think it will be safer to wait for Jack."

"He may not be here for some time—"

"'Sh! There he is now."

Just then the undergrowth separated behind
them, and the Indian joined them. He saw what
the matter was before they spoke.

"Stay here," he whispered. "I will look."

"What do you think of it?" asked Ned.

"There is some one in it," was the answer of the Mohawk, as he moved cautiously in the direction of the canoe.

CHAPTER XXXI.

A TEST OF THE NERVES.

By what means the Mohawk decided that the canoe resting so quietly against the bank contained some person, was more than Ned Clinton and Jo Minturn could tell, until he stopped a moment to explain.

"Boat sink low in water—too low itself—some one sink it!"

This, then, was the simple manner by which he judged. The vessel was lower than it would have been were there not something more than its own weight to cause the depression.

"Stay here," added the Mohawk. "Me go see."

The youths remained in a stationary position, while the veteran moved down the shore in the direction of the canoe, his friends watching his actions with a painful intensity of interest. They saw him advance step by step, never once removing his eyes from the boat, in which he was sure either a friend or enemy was

234

lying. When he reached the point within a couple of rods, he paused, and stood for a full minute in a crouching posture, scrutinizing the canoe as though he had discovered the identity of its occupant. Then, instead of keeping on down the shore, he stepped into the water, wading out until it reached to his knees, when he resumed his march upon the craft.

He did not reach it—that is, close enough to touch the gunwale with his hand, but the spectators were sure that he went nigh enough to see who was within. And then, to the unbounded amazement of the two lads, he began retreating, walking backward, till he made the point where he entered the river, when he stepped out and rapidly rejoined them. They looked in his face, hoping to read some explanation of his singular course, but they might as well have studied the countenance of a bronze image.

"Is there any one in the canoe?" asked Ned, resolved that the Mohawk should explain what he meant by his actions.

"Yes—some one there."

"Who is he?"

Lena-Wingo turned and looked directly in the

face of the speaker without uttering a word in reply, for several seconds. Then he said:

"You young scout—brave man?"

"Well, I don't know about that," was the rather confused reply of the blushing Ned.

"Yes, you brave man—go kill him!"

He accompanied these startling words by pointing toward the boat, so there could be no mistake as to his meaning. Having discovered the occupant of the canoe asleep and unconscious, he left him there, when he had him at his mercy, and took the trouble to come back and give the lad the task of putting him out of the way. A nice duty, indeed!

But Ned resolved that he would not back out, repulsive as it was.

War is made up of cruelty, and, in fighting these redmen and Tories, it was a weak sentimentality that showed them mercy, after what they had done to the settlers. Such was the argument with which Ned strove to convince himself that it was his duty to steal up to the sleeping warrior and bury his knife in his body! He did not stop to reflect that the Mohawk was noted for displaying mercy in the same direction; but, having already received more than one compliment from him, he could not afford to forfeit his good opinion now by any exhibition of timidity when asked to perform so simple a task as that of putting a redskin to his eternal sleep.

"I'll do it, Jack," he said, straightening up, with the resolution written on every line of his countenance; "I'll do it for *you*."

The Mohawk nodded his head in a way to show that he was pleased with the grit displayed by the youth, and he muttered:

"Brave boy—kill him—do it well."

"Shall I shoot him, or use the knife?"

"No shoot—Iroquois will hear—use knife—won't hear."

"If that is to be the way to manage the thing, I may as well leave my gun behind, as it will only be in the way."

"Yes; leave gun—take knife."

The reason for this was probably because the gun would be an encumbrance, when there was no expectation of using it. If he carried nothing but the knife, he would not be tempted to use any other weapon, and it meant the most serious kind of work.

"I would n't do it," whispered Jo, noticing that his friend was on the point of starting.

"Of course I will," replied Ned, in the same
guarded voice. "He wouldn't ask me unless he
had good reason for it."

At this juncture, when the young scout was
about to set out, he took the hunting-knife in his
grasp, but the Mohawk interfered.

"Don't do that," he said, "put in waist—get it
when want it."

Ned obeyed him without hesitation, shoving it
down in the top of his trousers, with the handle
projecting upward, so that it could be withdrawn
at any instant desired. All being ready, the young
scout made a start, unaware that at the same
second the Mohawk played a rather curious trick
upon him. With a quick, dexterous movement,
Lena-Wingo drew out the knife again, doing it so
neatly, indeed, that Jo failed to observe it. With
the same dexterity he concealed it about his person, where it could not attract the attention of
any one.

Thus it was that Ned Clinton actually set out
to "finish" an Indian warrior, without any
weapon with which to do it. Ned had the advantage of the example of the Mohawk scout to guide
him in his approach to the canoe containing the
sleeping redskin, and he did his best to imitate

his every movement. He made his way with the same consummate caution as did he, until he reached the spot where the savage went into the water, when he also stepped into the current, the depth of which he knew from having noticed it when waded by his friend.

It was necessary, after having started, that he should give his entire attention to the boat which he was approaching. There was the danger that the sleeping redskin might awake, in which case the situation of the young scout would not be the most desirable in the world; for, if the lad had really possessed his knife, as he supposed he did, it could have served him no purpose until he got within close range, while the redskin would have the advantage of a shot from his rifle. But this contingency caused Ned little fear, for he knew that his two friends behind him were watching every step he took, and if such a thing should happen, the Mohawk would save him.

The closer the lad drew to the canoe, the greater became his caution, until his progress was very slow, and it seemed to Jo more than once that he had actually paused and was standing still. But the young scout was advancing all the time, and he was now within a few steps of the boat. His heart beat so violently that he was afraid he would be betrayed by that means alone, for he knew that no person sleeps more lightly than the Indian. He wondered again and again why it was this warrior lay so still, when he must have known, before lying down, that he placed himself in great peril. However, the courage of the lad never faltered. The Mohawk had given him the task to do, and if it were within the range of human possibility, he meant it should be done.

It was a severe test of one's nerves thus to steal up to a deadly foe, with the intention that actuated him. As the boy recalled his experience of the last few days, he was sure there was nothing in it at all to equal this—not even when he was making his way through the Susquehanna, with the enemies in the front and rear. But his nerves, tense as they were, became as steel, when at last he reached a point from which he caught a glimpse of the bright garments of the occupant.

The young scout concluded that this was the time for him to draw his knife, so as to have it ready to use the next moment. Accordingly he reached his hand down, when the cold perspiration sprang out all over his body, for it was gone. He paused as if smitten by a bullet from the foe whom he was approaching, for here he was, and powerless to help himself.

CHAPTER XXXII.

THE OCCUPANT OF THE CANOE.

CLINTON stood transfixed. The disappointment was so unexpected, so unprepared for, that he was as powerless as a child in the presence of some overwhelming danger. Had the Indian arisen at that moment, he would have found an easy victim in the youth, who had set out with such high courage. Ned never dreamed that the Mohawk had anything to do with the disappearance of his weapon, nor would he have believed it, unless he had himself witnessed the purloining.

A few seconds were sufficient to recover his self-possession, and, supposing that he had dropped the knife while stealing along with such care, he turned about to go back and secure another. As he did so, he saw Jo and Lena-Wingo looking at him, and it seemed their faces were not as serious as they ought to be at such a time. The Indian motioned for him to go ahead—a piece of advice which the lad could

not appreciate, and he hesitated to obey it. But
Jo, at this juncture, joined him in signaling the
same thing, and, fearful that their purpose
might not be understood, he actually said, in a
voice which was distinctly heard by the aston-
ished Ned:

"Take a look at him! Take a look at him!"

"That's queer business," growled young
Clinton. "They must think that warrior is
sleeping like a log, to keep it up with all this
racket about him."

However, he concluded to gratify their whim,
and he moved carefully back until he was closer
than before—so nigh, indeed, that he was able
to see the occupant of the canoe. Occupant it
certainly had, in the person of the dearest object
on earth—Miss Rosa Minturn.

She was reclining with her brilliantly-colored
shawl gathered about her, and sleeping as
quietly as an infant, with no sign that any
hostile Indian knew anything of her whereabouts. One cheek rested on her arm, while the
other was turned to the mild summer breeze
that was stealing over the Susquehanna. With
her shawl drawn about her shoulders, the picture

of sleeping innocence and beauty was as winning
as could be.

The revulsion from his grim and gloomy state
of mind, caused by the discovery that instead of a
fierce, painted redskin stretched in the bottom of
the boat was the enchanting object of his affection, was so great that he could barely prevent
himself from uttering a cry of joy, and he stood
for several minutes gazing in silent rapture on the
picture. He was roused by hearing the voice of
his friend Jo:

"I'm afraid you'll catch cold, Ned, if you stand
all the afternoon in the water."

The young man turned his head and saw them
both laughing, the grin of the Mohawk especially
being of tremendous proportions. Through the
strange and apparently contradictory nature of
Lena-Wingo ran a vein of humor, which showed
itself at the most unexpected times, and no one
could have enjoyed the astonishment of Ned more
than did he on the present occasion.

"Bring the boat here," called out Jo, when the
thing had lasted several minutes. "What's the
use of leaving it there?"

This was a sensible suggestion, and Ned acted

upon it at once by reaching out his hand, seizing the gunwale, and moving up-stream with it.

"Here's your knife," said Jo, with a laugh, as he handed the weapon to him. "The next time you start on such an expedition as that, you had better take something of the kind along."

"That's some of your or Lena-Wingo's work," replied Ned, feeling that the joke was at his expense, and very willing to bear it, when the result was so in consonance with the best wishes and prayers of his heart.

They might have laughed for an hour, for all he cared, so long as the missing girl was restored to them. Reaching the point where his friends were waiting him, he drew the canoe well up the bank, so there was no danger of its floating away, while Jo explained the little trick that the Mohawk played upon his friend.

"She sleeps soundly," said the brother, leaning over, and gently touching his lips to the warm cheek of the girl. "Poor sister, she so required rest that she forgot herself, and went to sleep when she didn't mean to; but no harm is done."

It was deemed best not to disturb her for the present, as she was in need of the slumber she was enjoying, and was quite certain to awake in

a short time. Lena-Wingo explained that he suspected the girl was asleep in the canoe the instant
he saw the boat lying against the bank; for, as it
was plain that some one was within, nothing
was more likely than it was the one that had
gone away with the boat. There was the possibility, however, that such was not the case,
and before carrying out his little joke, he made
sure of the truth. When he saw that Rosa was
found, he arranged the jest for his own amusement, carrying it out with the success which we
have already shown to our readers.

The friends were conversing in guarded under-
tones, when there was a rustle from the boat, and
looking in that direction, Rosa was seen in a sitting position, looking inquiringly upon them, as if
she did not exactly understand what it all meant.

"Well, my sister, we have taken you prisoner,
after you tried so hard to give us the slip,"
remarked Jo, with a laugh.

"It looked once as though we should be unable
to find you at all," added Ned, extending his hand
to help her from the boat to the shore. "We made
a hunt for you, and Jo and I were about ready to
give up, when we caught sight of the canoe."

Rosa reached out her hand in response to the proffer of her young admirer, but she sprang as lightly ashore as a bird—scarcely needing the help given her. Not entirely disappointed was Ned, for when the fairy fingers lightly touched his own, the thrill that went through the system of the young scout was like that from the electric battery. The crimson flush stole over his face, and he was sure that all would laugh at his embarrassment, but nobody seemed to notice it, and he soon recovered his self-possession, as the group seated themselves together, on the leaves, just far enough withdrawn from the river to avoid being seen by any that might be going up or down stream.

"And this is what you call waiting for me?" was the half-serious question of Jo Minturn to his sister, when they were seated.

"I promised to wait for you if I could, didn't I?" she said, in reply.

"Well, and what was there to hinder?"

"Three Iroquois—was not that enough?"

"It will do, if there is nothing better to offer; but I don't understand how you could get away from three Indians by jumping into a canoe and paddling such a short way."

"How can you, when I haven't explained?"

"I'll be glad to learn."

"It was only a short time after you left that I heard signals very near me in the woods. I knew they were made by some of the Iroquois scouts that were prowling in the neighborhood, though what they were after was more than I could tell, for it didn't seem likely they were hunting for me. I didn't doubt, however, that they would stop to pick me up if they got the chance, so I kept watch on them. In a little while I saw one of them to the right, and, as he was moving toward me, I thought it time to see whether the way was open on the left yonder; but I hadn't gone far, when I found there was an Indian stealing from that direction, while there was the best reason to suspect a third one was almost as near as they. Well, I began to think I was in a bad situation, and there wasn't much prospect of getting out by pushing ahead, so I moved back toward the Susquehanna, uncertain what I would do when I got there, but well satisfied that it was the only way open. The first thing that caught my eye on reaching the river was the canoe lying against the bank, as it must have been all the time without our suspecting it."

CHAPTER XXXIII.

THE CONSULTATION.

"THAT canoe," continued Rosa, "must have been sent by Heaven itself. I felt it the instant I caught sight of it. I knew that if I staid here any longer the Iroquois would catch me; so I stepped into the boat, and shoved it clear of the shore. There was no paddle, and I hadn't time to look around to see where it had been hid. That stopped me from going out in the river, too, though I don't know as I would have done that if the oar was there—that is, unless they pursued me, and there was no other way of escaping. I dropped down along the shore, keeping as close as I could, and allowing the canoe to drift with the current, which you know runs very slow so close in. I kept it up awhile, stopping now and then to listen; but I heard nothing, and when it seemed to me that I had gone far enough, I drew it to the bank, and sat down to listen and watch for the redmen. Well, I must have fallen asleep, for I don't remember anything until I woke up a few minutes ago. I know that I was very sleepy, for I didn't get one minute's slumber last night, and it's hard to do nothing but sit still and keep awake at such a time."

No one present could criticise the course of the fair fugitive, whose action had, doubtless, saved her from falling into the hands of the Iroquois when they were so close upon her. There was so much general joy over the reunion that there was no room for fault-finding with each other, especially when there was so little cause for it.

The long summer afternoon of the day which, like the preceding, was to live in their memories as among the most eventful of all their lives, was far advanced, and night would soon be upon them. Before holding a full consultation as to future plans and course of action, the Mohawk made a reconnoissance of their own position, for the purpose of learning whether there was immediate danger of any of the Iroquois breaking in upon them. He returned in less than half an hour, declaring that nothing of the kind was to be apprehended, and the four sat down to a conversation which was a freer one than they had enjoyed since starting upon their memorable journey.

Precisely what they were to do was left, as may be supposed, to the Mohawk, under whose guidance they all placed themselves. It did not take him long to tell what he had decided upon. His purpose was to wait where they were, or, perhaps, near there, till night was fully upon them, and then to cross the river to the other shore and make their way to Wilkesbarre.

It was stated at the opening of our story that, during the massacre which succeeded the battle of Wyoming, a panic seized the garrison and settlers at Wilkesbarre. Believing the victorious Indians and Tories were about to cross over and massacre them all, a stampede took place in the direction of Stroudsburg and other points, many of the fugitives starting in such haste that a great number perished by the way—the wilderness where the fatality was so frightful, being known to this day as the "Shades of Death." This panic was unwarranted. Those who remained were safe from molestation, since Colonel Butler and his allies were too nearly defeated as it was, at Wyoming, to incur any risk of having the tables turned upon him.

Lena-Wingo understood the situation, and was well satisfied that they had only to make the point named to be beyond the reach of their enemies. His plan, therefore, was the most simple that could be devised, and it needed scarcely any explanation from him, when he had once intimated it to his friends. As he had done once before that day, he declared that it was important that they should find some means of providing themselves with food before undertaking to finish the journey, speaking of course in this matter more for his companions than for himself.

It was useless to protest against such a course, when the Mohawk had made up his mind to it. No doubt he believed that Rosa felt the need of food, and he was determined she should have it; and it may be supposed that after his experience of the afternoon, there was no likelihood of his repeating the blunder then made.

A stillness like that of the great solitude itself fell upon them as they sat in the dense undergrowth of the woods, talking in low tones of their future plans, and speculating as to what their enemies were doing at that time. The Mohawk took no part in the words that passed between them. He was inclined to reticence at all times, and rarely spoke except when there was necessity therefor, or when he had some of his little schemes

for his own amusement on hand. Leaving the
others to do the chatting, he busied himself in
searching for the paddle reported missing by Rosa
Minturn. As may be imagined, it did not take
him long to find where it had been placed beneath
some dry leaves.

"Now, if that boat was left here by a redskin,
as must have been the case," said Ned Clinton,
"why, is it not likely that the owner will be back
before long to take charge of it again?"

"I have thought of the same thing more than
once," replied Jo, "but I concluded that if Jack
was satisfied we ought to be."

The Mohawk was absent at that moment and
Rosa added:

"Lena-Wingo is likely to make mistakes the
same as any one else, for all he is the smartest
man I ever saw in the woods. If he had n't
insisted on going in that deserted house, and sitting down to eat, we would n't have got into the
trouble we did."

"But he managed to get out of it again," said
Ned Clinton.

"But he would have had hard work, if it
had n't been for *you*," remarked Jo Minturn.

"I don't know about that," Ned was equally prompt to say. "I was able to do something, it is true, to hurry up matters, but you know there isn't any scrape that the Mohawk can't manage to pull out of in some way or other, and, if I hadn't come along just as I did, he would have outwitted the Iroquois in one way or another."

"Well," replied Jo, impatiently, "suppose we say that you never did anything at all; that, I guess, will suit you better, for I don't undertake to tell anything about you that you don't put in a protest. How will that suit Ned?"

"That will do well enough," he answered, with a laugh. "I am not hunting after honor that doesn't belong to me."

"And aren't willing to take that which does belong to you, either."

"I wonder what has become of Jack," said Ned, turning his head, and looking off in the gathering twilight; "I don't like to have him gone too long."

"He is looking after our interests," replied Rosa; "I remember when we used to go hunting and had to camp in the woods, he was on the go all the time. He would sit down a while, and when we were talking, would jump up and be off like a shot. When he came back, he tried to make me believe he had heard some kind of game in the forest, but I was sure he was telling a fib half the time, and only wanted an excuse for leaving me as he did."

"You may be sure he is within call," said Ned, "and, if anything turns up demanding his presence, he will be back in a twinkling; but, for all that, I wish he were here."

"Do you know," said Jo, looking at the couple, with a glowing face, "that I consider our adventures, or at least our dangers, over?"

"And why do you think that?" inquired his sister, with some surprise.

"This is the first time all of us have been together. So long as we were separated, some or every one was in danger. But now we are under the care of the smartest Indian in the country; we have weapons and ammunition, and he will soon lead us to a place of safety, where we can stay until all peril is over."

Ned and Rosa caught the contagion of the youth's buoyancy of spirits, and came to believe that their stirring experiences were ended, and that soon all would be well with them and the loved ones not far away. They therefore awaited the return of the Mohawk in a more tranquil and comfortable state of mind than at any time since the invasion of the Wyoming valley by the Tories and Indians.

THE END.

www.ingramcontent.com/pod-product-compliance
Lightning Source LLC
Chambersburg PA
CBHW031424020726
47499CB00005B/1592